Real Ghost Stories:
True Tales Of The
Supernatural
From The UK

Volume Two

TINA VANTYLER

The items in this anthology have been drawn from interviews or inspired by genuine events. To protect the privacy of individuals, names, identifying details and the exact locations of events have been changed. Any resemblance to actual persons, living or dead, or actual places is entirely coincidental. Similarly, any perceived slight to persons or organisations is not intended and the author and publisher shall have no liability or responsibility whatsoever should these arise. The information in this book is for entertainment purposes only. The author and publisher shall have no liability or responsibility for the consequences of actions or interpretations by persons taken as a response to the material in this book.

Published by Zanderam London Press
First printing 2021
ISBN: 978-1-7399072-0-4
Copyright © 2021, Tina Vantyler
Website: tinavantylerbooks.com
Cover design by Martellia

CONTENTS

Introduction		1
1.	Someone To Watch Over Me	5
2.	Bad Vibrations	19
3.	Bonded By Blood	33
4.	Room 18	43
5.	Mum's The Word	50
6.	Cold Comfort	59
7.	Victor Victorious	62
8.	Shipshape	70
9.	Different Strokes	77
10.	All Keyed Up	83
11.	Crowded House	93
12.	Height Of Despair	100
13.	School's Out	110

14. Up In Smoke   124

15. A Rational Man   131

Newsletter & Free Novella   135

Also by Tina Vantyler   138

INTRODUCTION

***Ready For 15 Thrilling, Chilling
Original True Ghost Stories?***

WELCOME TO MY SECOND book of true ghost stories
from the UK, a nation that boasts centuries-old traditions
of paranormal tales both real and fictional.

When I started on this journey of chatting to people
from all walks of life about their encounters with the
supernatural, while I've long been intrigued by the occult,
I was something of a sceptic where ghosts were concerned.

With a background in psychology and journalism, I
wasn't quite convinced that there really were entities that
make themselves known to the living, and which we
call ghosts. This was even after I had my own frightful
experience, the story of which I included in my first book,
*Real Ghost Stories: True Tales Of The Supernatural From
The UK*.

That view has changed. After talking to 15 more people

for this volume and hearing their accounts, from those who believe they've lived alongside ghosts for decades to individuals who had a one-off spectral encounter, I am utterly convinced that the events of which they speak took place.

Even so, after telling me their tale, several said, 'I know you'll probably think I'm crazy...'

Well... for me, the explanation offered by Edgar, an engineer and former Naval officer who contributed a tale to this collection, about why some people experience the supernatural while others don't, rings true. As he reminds us, humans only see a small part of the light spectrum, we hear within a limited frequency compared to, for example, dogs and bats, and radar signals, electricity and radio signals are invisible to us. 'We have quite a narrow bandwidth, or range, that we're aware of,' he says. 'But I think some people have a wider bandwidth than others, and whether I like it or not, that seems to include me.' (You can read about Edgar's nightmarish experiences at sea in his story, *Shipshape*.)

Quite a few of the folk who generously shared their stories with me have had several supernatural confrontations. And no, I don't think they're crazy. On the contrary, it seems they have something we ordinary folk don't – an unusually wide 'bandwidth'.

Even if you haven't come across a phantom yet, that doesn't mean you never will. Single encounters are incredibly common and I suspect no one is completely immune to a persistent spirit. Maybe reading tales such as these help to open your mind, making you more susceptible, especially in the dead of night...

Appointment With Fear

Now we come to the stories. All original and hand-picked for their unique and uncanny nature, you won't find these 15 unearthly tales anywhere else.

Ready for a deliciously thrilling, chilling read? If only in your mind, darkness falls within and without, a fire burns merrily in the grate and the clock strikes midnight. So light a candle to set the atmosphere and chase away those shadows in the corners, settle comfortably in your chair and venture with me into a world of genuine heart-stopping encounters with phantoms and poltergeists.

Prepare to have your dreams haunted by the ghastly images in stories such as:

- The activity that terrified a paranormal investigator in *Bad Vibrations*...

- The former funeral parlour's foul visitor in *Up In*

Smoke...

- The battle between feminine energy and masculine malevolence in *Someone To Watch Over Me...*

- The marrow-freezing expression of affection in *Different Strokes...*

- The bloody pact that led to pandemonium in *Bonded By Blood...*

Be sure to check the gloomy space under your bed tonight before stepping into it – if your clammy hands can hold a torch after you've sampled these sinister stories, that is...

ONE

SOMEONE TO WATCH OVER ME

The dream cottage was Jemma and Aaron's first home together. But was it his clandestine conduct that led events to take a nightmarish turn?

A COUPLE OF DECADES ago, when I was in my 20s, my fiancé Aaron and me were thrilled to buy a detached cottage in Pembrokeshire as our first home. An old farmer's house with two bedrooms, it had been empty for a year and had become derelict, with smashed windows, black mould growing up the walls and no kitchen to speak of. We began renovating it and the first signs that it was haunted came when we put a partition wall in upstairs to split one of the bedrooms into two.

We'd just built the wooden framework but hadn't nailed the plasterboard sheets on. Having left the hammer and screwdrivers sitting on a bar of the wooden frame for the night, Aaron and I were downstairs watching TV.

It must have been around 8pm when there was a loud

crash in the partitioned room above our heads.

I took the stairs two at a time with Aaron behind me.

The screwdrivers and hammer were on the other side of the room.

'How is that possible?' exclaimed Aaron. 'They couldn't have fallen off and ended up all the way over there. It looks as though someone picked them up and carried them.'

'Or rather threw them with some force, given the noise it made,' I replied, picking the items up. 'Strange!' I placed them on the floor by the frame and we returned to our TV programme.

That happened four or five times and, believe it or not, we laughed the events off and simply got used to them. Aaron and I were quite chilled people – initially, that is, anyway.

He worked in London part of the week, so I was often alone in the house, which was fine by me. Although isolated, the setting was idyllic. The place stood in a pretty wooded valley that was part of a forest, and we were also by the coast, with a lane that led down to the beach. Our nearest neighbour was a tiny church about quarter of a mile away, which was usually deserted. There were no streetlights and it was as black as tar after nightfall – so dark that you could put your hand in front of your face and not be able to see it.

One night when Aaron was in London, I was asleep upstairs when I suddenly jerked awake. An old lady was standing next to the bed, kind of hunched over. She was wearing a white cotton Victorian nightgown that had an embroidered square on the front with lace around it, and a close-fitting lace cap. I just knew that under the cap, she had long grey hair tied up in a bun. In her hand, she held a candle in its holder, the flickering, golden flame illuminating her figure. The woman was looking straight into my face but, astonishingly, I wasn't scared. On the contrary, her presence gave me a warm, comforting feeling.

I started to get out of bed and as I rose, the woman disappeared. I didn't see her disappear or fade; she simply wasn't there anymore. I didn't tell Aaron about this and we carried on with our life there as normal.

A couple of months in, we were off to visit family and because the place was so isolated, I didn't want to leave my jewellery out in case we were burgled. So Aaron took off the cover we'd made for the hall radiator, stowed the box in there and fastened the cover back on.

Days later, we were back home and I asked Aaron to get the jewellery box. Not wanting to unscrew the radiator cover, he dug around in the gap at the back, trying to pull my jewellery out piece by piece. 'No, I want the actual box, please!' I said impatiently. 'Don't be so lazy!'

So he unscrewed the cover, took out the box and gave it me. Thanks to his rummaging, my necklaces, earrings and rings were all tangled together.

I took the box upstairs and laid it on the pine dresser. 'What a mess he's made of my precious jewellery,' I thought, looking at the jumble of chains and metal. 'I'll sort it out later.' I closed the lid and went down to dinner.

Later, I went up to bed and, walking into the room, I noticed something was different. On the dresser, the jewellery box lid was open. All my necklaces were laid out beside it, stretched to their full length, one above another. My earrings were next to them, arranged in pairs. My rings had been placed carefully in the foam ring spaces in the box.

Aaron appeared at my back. 'Er... thanks for tidying my jewellery,' I said, although I had an odd feeling about the situation.

'First of all, you know me, I certainly couldn't be arsed to lay it all out like that,' he replied. 'Plus, didn't you notice? I haven't been upstairs all evening. We've been together in the lounge ever since you took the box up.'

That's when I told him about the lady I'd seen in our bedroom. 'I think this is her doing,' I said. 'I get the feeling she's looking after me.'

'Can't say I'm keen on the idea of this old girl knocking

around, but if you reckon she's here and you don't mind, then neither do I,' he said, squeezing my shoulder affectionately.

After that, nothing much happened for a while but I could sense the lady's energy around the place, kind energy. And you'll think this sounds really weird, but from then on, when we had a roast dinner, and at Christmas, we would set a place for her at the dining table to make her feel welcome.

Luckily, she never took advantage of our hospitality by showing up, but I like to think she appreciated the gesture.

Unfortunately, after we'd been there a couple of years, whatever it was that was in the house with us began to turn nasty.

The two of us were renovating the living room and it had a huge, dusty carpet from the 1950s or 60s, a good quality one, so we'd kept it. Today, we lifted it up to find four mummified mice stuck to the underside.

'Euw!' I said, coughing at the rising dust. 'They're all flat from the pressure of the carpet. Pretty disturbing.'

We looked at the tiny stiff bodies, each with four legs outstretched and a shrivelled, curving tail.

'Maybe there were cats here and the mice hid and got stuck,' mused Aaron, bringing over a dustpan and brush to scoop the corpses into. 'Look – there are patches of loose threads along the edge of the carpet that might have been done by a cat. They do shred carpets, to sharpen their claws. Our one at home would do that.'

'Remember that old doormat we chucked?' I said. 'From by the front door? That was practically in ribbons and there were all those deep scratches along the wooden step inside. Same cat?'

It was a bit unsettling, but we made a bonfire in the garden that afternoon and burned the carpet and dried mice. We thought nothing more about it but who knows, maybe that had something to do with what happened a few weeks later.

Aaron was away and I was in our back bedroom. Drifting up from a deep sleep, I became aware there was a lot of noise in the room. It sounded like the spitting, snarling and yowling of angry cats fighting.

I was lying on my back. 'OK, I'm dreaming,' I thought. 'All the doors are locked and there are no cats here.' As I opened my eyes to full wakefulness, the sounds faded and the room fell silent.

Then the unthinkable happened.

The room was in total blackness, but I felt what I knew was a cat on my feet. It started to walk up me from the bottom of the bed, and its paws kept slipping in between my legs because of the duvet. As the animal moved slowly up to my stomach, one step at a time, I felt a second cat on my pillow, winding itself back and forth around the top of my head. Hot terror rose in my throat but, even in my horror, somehow I knew that the cat walking up my body was ginger with a white paw and the one by my head was a tabby with three white feet. I was rigid with fear, my hands flat to the bed on either side of me but I could feel the cats' tails waving around in the darkness.

Finding my strength, I jumped out of bed, planning to rush to the door, which was shut. But then I stopped. The hall light, switched off by me earlier, had flashed on. The angry cat noises began again outside the door, then I saw the shadow of four legs as if another cat was pacing the width of my door outside, up and down, up and down. That one was really irate, switching its tail this way and that, and I knew it was black, with two white front paws. On my bed, the other cats had gone.

Then the light went out, the room was dark once again and I ran to the door, shaking and with tears running down my cheeks, absolutely petrified, for the first and only time ever in my life. I put all the lights in the house on and sat downstairs with my duvet around me for the rest of the night.

It was incredibly scary but I didn't tell anyone about it – not even Aaron. Something made me want to keep the incident to myself. Then several weeks later, I met an elderly lady walking down our lane who said she had a house nearby and was collecting dandelions for her tortoises. I can't remember how the conversation started, but we got chatting and I asked her about our house.

'It belonged to Maud, who was in her eighties,' she said. 'Died what, three years ago now.'

I'd heard something of this – I knew the lady who had owned our house had been a heavy drinker and had collapsed in the hall but hadn't died there. The church caretaker had told us this – he'd found her and called the ambulance, and she'd passed away in hospital.

'Maud was a kind, friendly lady, but she had such a problem with alcohol,' the woman continued. 'She wasn't a very nice person when she'd had a drink. But it's lovely that a young couple have moved in. Maud fed the birds every day – do you like birds? She loved them. She'd get so angry with her cats though, because, being cats, they'd chase the birds away, or catch them and bring the dead bodies to the house.'

My stomach dropped. 'How many cats did Maud have?' I asked.

'Three – a ginger one, a tabby–'

I interrupted her. 'Did the tabby have three white paws?'

'Yes,' she said. 'And the third one was black. That was

Cosmo.'

'Did Cosmo have white paws?' I asked.

'He did,' she smiled. 'Two. Lovely animals, they were.'

I was gasping and she looked at me curiously. 'You've seen a picture of the cats, then?'

'No...' I wasn't going to tell her about my encounter with the creatures.

Things in the house got worse and worse after that. I later found out that Aaron had reasons other than work to keep heading off to London – he'd started having an affair roundabout the time we found the dead mice under the carpet.

By now, I'd got a house rabbit to keep me company, a big French Lop called Podge – my gentle giant. It was evening and I was in the living room – I remember I was watching the game show *Shooting Stars* on TV and chuckling away to myself. Podge was snoozing in front of me on the rug with his back legs stretched out behind him – his usual position. Aaron was down the hallway in the bath – the bathroom was downstairs, quite a way from the lounge. The living room door was shut. Then the handle moved slightly, enough to make little metallic clicks, as though someone was trying to open it.

Next, from just outside the door, a man's voice roared, 'FUCK OFF!' I jumped and Podge leaped 3ft off the floor, shot the doorway a wild-eyed look and sped behind the sofa. I ran to the door and tore it open. Finding the hall empty, I rushed down to the bathroom.

Still in the tub, Aaron turned to me as I opened the door. No way would he have had time to run to the lounge, yell and get back to his bath. He looked startled. 'Before you ask, no, that shout wasn't me and I know it wasn't you,' he said. 'Perhaps it was your old lady's boyfriend.'

'This place is doing my head in,' I heard him mutter as I went to the lounge to get a cuddle from Podge.

Horrible things were happening daily now and I was starting to feel more and more frightened, especially as my fiancé was often away most of the week. We'd put in a little balcony upstairs overlooking the hall and once, alone in the house, when I was walking down the stairs, I could feel someone following my movements from the balcony with their eyes. I was too scared to look around and I had that same feeling a couple of times out in the garden, this time that I was being observed from an upstairs window. Again, I didn't dare turn to check.

Strangely, I began to get the impression there was a man about the house watching me, and although I hadn't actually seen him, I was fully aware of what he looked like – it's hard to explain how I knew. He was well dressed, in a waistcoat, with a hat like a small bowler on his head. He was stern, an authoritarian, old Victorian type. I 'saw' him maybe five times around the house. I believe it was him who swore so viciously that night.

Unbeknown to me, Aaron was five months into his affair by now. It was summer, and one afternoon, we went down the hill to a little tearoom. I'd popped in once before, but only stood on the doorstep.

We were sitting in the back having tea and, over Aaron's shoulder on the wall, I could see framed photos of the local area. Our cottage was one of a spread-out group of old dwellings, and there were pictures of them all, along with plaques outlining the history of the district. I couldn't believe my eyes when I spotted one picture. It was black and white and there, standing outside our place, was the man I'd 'seen' in the house. He was holding the hand of a boy of about five years old, who was clutching a teddy bear.

As I sat there Aaron said, 'Jemma, what's wrong? All the colour has drained from your face.' But I couldn't speak, because there was so much I hadn't told him, although he knew that something had been going on upstairs when the tools were thrown and my jewellery was rearranged right at the start. Obviously I'd said a bit about the old lady, but that was it.

Now I said, 'Behind you. You see that man posing in

front of our house? Well, I've seen him. In the house.'

Aaron shot me a look of contempt. He'd already checked out of our relationship emotionally – I can see that now. 'You're just making it up,' he snapped. 'Of course you haven't seen this guy.'

We used to be so close, but now it didn't take much to make Aaron annoyed with me.

I do feel there was a connection between the awful things that began to happen in the house and the fact Aaron had started playing away.

I suspect his cheating brought bad energy into the building. We had dreadful fights and it was horrendous. Silent calls to the house phone started, which I later discovered was the woman Aaron was seeing. I found out what he'd been up to and threw him out of the house. But yes, the old lady wanted to protect me well before I knew what Aaron was doing – before he even started the affair. She was looking out for me – that's the feeling I got from early on. Could she have known he was about to betray me? And did something about Aaron's affair block her feminine vibrations and allowed the grim man's dark, masculine spirit to take over?

There's some confusion in my mind as to the identity of the lady I saw in my room. I never thought to ask for a photo of the woman with the cats who'd died a year before we bought the place. My feeling was that it was her who'd been caring for me, but then the person in my bedroom had definitely been dressed in period clothes. Did she have some positive emotional link to Maud? My sense now is that the lady in white was Maud's mother or grandmother.

Aaron and me were in that house two and a half years and, after we'd sold up, I moved to the country on my own. Having done some research since, I understand I'm what's known as a Highly Sensitive Person, which means I process information more deeply than others and am unusually sensitive to my environment and other people's emotions. I have memories from when I was a child of being aware of things I couldn't possibly have known by normal means. Today, out and about, or walking in the woods with my dog, I can meet people – strangers – and sense when they need comfort or support.

One last thing. When everything had fallen apart with Aaron and I'd put the house on the market and moved in with a friend, I popped back one day to gather some items.

I was in the garden packing the outdoor chairs when I spotted the lady who owned the tortoises strolling by with her dandelion basket. She came over when she saw me.

'I noticed the *For Sale* sign,' she sighed. 'You're young, and I can understand that maybe this place is too remote for the pair of you.'

I explained that the relationship had run its course, but not about the problems in the house.

'I meant to ask,' I said. 'What happened to Maud's cats? Did someone adopt them?'

A shadow crossed the woman's face. 'No. It was ever so sad. Maud was taken to hospital and everyone forgot about the cats. I was away. We didn't know, but the cats were locked in the house. They died there – starved to nothing. The mat at the front door had been all torn and pulled loose where they'd clawed at it and tried to get out.'

I'd suffered terribly in that house. But I felt sick and weepy thinking about what those cats had been through.

TWO

BAD VIBRATIONS

Leela has witnessed a stream of supernatural incidents. But the events in her student house were even too frightening for a top paranormal investigator to deal with...

I'VE EXPERIENCED ALL MANNER of mystical things, so I'll describe just the main ones. I only saw what I think was a ghost on one occasion though, when I was very young.

I was six, in my bed in the house my mum, dad and brother still live in. It was summer, and you know how it gets light really early in the morning? I'd been asleep and I don't know what woke me, but I opened my eyes and it was light, probably around 5am. Straight ahead of me, at the end of my bed, was a figure. It was sideways on and looked like a nun, dressed in black with a long headdress covering the head. Below that was a tunic with wide, baggy sleeves and a bulky skirt.

Initially, the thing was still, but then it took a step along the end of the bed, moving from left to right, still in profile and looking straight ahead. Its back was to the window, its pale face in shadow, so I couldn't tell whether it was young or old. I can't tell you how scared I felt. Would it keep moving and come and touch me, or even attack me?

I didn't wait to see if it took a second step. Squeezing my eyes tight shut, I repeated in my head, 'It's not really there, it's not really there,' over and over.

I can't recall how long it took to fall back to sleep, but I vividly remember waking up later and thinking, 'I never want to see that again.' I moved rooms and even now, as an adult, I don't like to go in there on my own.

I appreciate that one could say maybe this was just a young child having a nightmare who opened her eyes and then closed them without realising she was dreaming. But I believe what I saw was real and that feeling has stayed with me many years later. It was absolutely beyond terrible.

My brother hadn't been born at that point – he's six years younger than me. I didn't mention it to my mum and dad, because I knew they wouldn't be interested – Indian families don't believe in that kind of thing. My brother has that bedroom now and I told him my tale when he was a teenager. He was alarmed, but he's never experienced anything like that in there so he doesn't worry about it.

Although I don't know the full history of my street, there was an important priory very close by for 400 years up until the mid-1500s and I do wonder if the nun had something to do with that.

So that was the first thing.

The second was when I was 17, strolling with my boyfriend in the woods near home. As we came to a clearing, another young couple were walking our way, about our age. The girl was wearing a navy leather jacket and jeans. I happened to look down and when I raised my eyes, they'd disappeared – in front of us in an open space.

'Where did they go?' asked my boyfriend. 'I blinked and they'd gone.'

'The couple?' I said. 'I have no idea.' There was nowhere for them to run to, but these were very old woods rumoured to have been a meeting place for witches' covens for centuries. My boyfriend and I were pretty disturbed by this. It was very, very strange indeed.

Then came the big event I wanted to talk about. It was when I was at university in London.

Me and my friends Rosie, Tarak and Ethan were second-year psychology students and we moved into a house together. Before we took the house, we went to look at it – it was in the East End of London.

The house backed onto a graveyard, which is never a good thing, but we didn't care about that. I know a fair number of houses down that road had been hit by bombs during World War Two.

But the first creepy thing that happened was when we went to view the house.

The landlady opened the door to us. In her sixties, she had tatty grey hair to her shoulders and wolfish, discoloured teeth and I know this sounds judgmental, but she struck me as unpleasantly witch-like. She introduced herself and told us the little timid man on the doorstep beside her was her husband.

Showing us into the lounge, her husband trailing behind her, all six of us sat down. The lounge had a coal fire – not an ordinary, open one, but a wood-burner with a glass door that was filthy with soot. Nailed on the wall to the side was a long metal rack for the fire tools – the coal scoop, tongs, shovel and poker, each hanging on their hooks.

The four of us were seated on the sofa and the woman began to describe the house.

'There's an outside toilet as well as an indoor one upstairs, four good-sized bedrooms and a coal cellar. The door to that is under the stairs,' she said, her lips and hands twitching as though she were agitated. She grinned widely, showing big teeth the colour of yellowing parchment.

'It sounds perfect,' we chorused, looking at each other.

No one was near the fireplace but, suddenly, all the fire

tools fell from their hooks, hitting the floor with a loud clatter.

'How could everything have dropped off its hook at once like that?' I asked. 'This house isn't haunted, is it?'

The woman gave what I can only describe as a witchy cackle.

'No, absolutely not. Definitely not,' she chuckled. Timid husband smiled nervously but said nothing.

'What did you make of that?' asked Tarak as we walked down the path.

'We'd have an easy journey to uni, it's a nice big house and it's not as if we'll have much to do with Mr and Mrs Hocus Pocus,' said Rosie. 'The falling fire tools were a coincidence. Let's take it.'

So we moved in and pretty soon, the strange things began.

In the first week, I went down to breakfast one morning to find the glass door of the wood-burner totally clean and clear – gleamingly so – rather than caked with black soot. That confused us – we agreed it had been as dirty as ever the night we moved in and none of us had touched it since.

Another day I was making dinner in the kitchen and there was an old-fashioned pressure cooker, which was there when we moved in, sitting on the side. We hadn't used it, so it's not as if there was pressure inside it.

As I walked past it, the lid jumped into the air a few centimetres, then clanged back down. 'Most peculiar,' I thought.

So many different things happened. There was a period of a few weeks when we felt a lot of physical vibrations in the house, especially in my room, which was at the top front of the building. You could actually see objects shaking.

One of our friends, Gemma, who lived two streets away, claimed to have some kind of psychic gift. In my room one afternoon, she said, 'This is a miserable house – can't you feel it, Leela?' Closing her eyes, probably for effect, she said, 'You know what – there's a little boy here who's really unhappy.'

I considered her something of a troubled soul, so didn't plan to take much notice of her pronouncement. 'Erm... I doubt that,' I said. 'Fancy some chocolate? Let's go to the kitchen.'

Gemma opened her eyes, then widened them in surprise. 'Leela,' she said, waving her hand to indicate behind me, 'what's with your wardrobe? Why is your hairspray bottle, you know, shaking?'

I turned to look. The wardrobe doors were open and it had a shelf at the top with a few toiletries on. Gemma was right. The other items around it were still, but my hairspray bottle was shuddering away like an anxious mouse. As we watched, a couple of other bottles joined in. Ever the scientist, I leaned over and shut the wardrobe door. 'My theory is that there's an underground tube train tunnel below us, and it makes objects shake sometimes,' I said firmly.

'Then the shaking would be just as violent all over the house,' Gemma said over her shoulder as I pushed her out of my room. 'I think you have a troublesome entity in here.'

Next, three of us were away for the weekend and Tarak was in the house by himself. On the Sunday morning he rang me, his voice rising with panic. 'I got up today to find the speakers in my room had been turned around to face the wall in the night!' he said. 'Let's ring Rosie and Ethan. Please come home – quick.'

We were all pretty scared by now, but we came back to support Tarak – and anyway, we had classes next day.

'Let's all sleep in my room tonight,' I said. 'Safety in numbers.'

'My girlfriend Petra is coming over, so I'm fine in my own room,' said Ethan.

At bedtime, Rosie and me climbed into my bed and Tarak arranged a pile of pillows and settled down on the floor.

'Night all,' I said, switching off the lamp. I could feel Rosie's elbow sticking in me but I was grateful she was there.

Soon, regular breathing from the floor told us that Tarak was asleep. 'Lucky him,' whispered Rosie in the dark.

'Yeah – but keep still, will you,' I said. 'We've got to get up early tomorrow and I need my sleep.'

'I'm not doing anything,' exclaimed Rosie. 'And anyway, *you* keep still. Are you cold? You're shaking!'

'Of course not – hang on!' I said. 'It's the bed!'

And it was. The whole of my double bed was vibrating, like one of those massage chairs you get in nail parlours nowadays. I opened my mouth to scream – then the movement stopped dead.

'Shut up, you two,' came grumpily from the floor. 'And stop jumping about.'

'There – you felt it too, Tarak!' cried Rosie. 'We weren't jumping – the bed was trembling.'

'I don't want to hear that,' said Tarak. 'Shush.'

A minute later in the silence, I heard a sound. Wood on wood, a kind of slow sliding that I couldn't identify at first. Then a rush of air, followed by a slam.

'That,' whispered Rosie, 'was a drawer opening and shutting, wasn't it?'

I twigged. 'Yes,' I hissed. 'And I know which one.

The top drawer of that old, built-in cupboard under the window.'

'And it's above my head!' exclaimed Tarak. 'I'm moving.' I heard him wriggle across the floor until he was close to my side of the bed.

'Let's get up,' said Rosie, putting a hand on my arm.

I was on my back, eyes shut. 'Hopefully that's it now,' I said. 'We'll deal with it tomorrow.'

Somehow, we all nodded off. At one point, I heard my door softly open, then it was pulled to. 'That'll be Ethan, checking to see what's going on,' I thought. 'Who can blame him? I bet we woke him up.'

Next day, around the breakfast table, both Tarak and Rosie said they also heard the bedroom door open and close.

'It wasn't me,' said Ethan. 'Why would I bother doing that? Me and Petra were fast asleep, weren't we?'

Petra nodded enthusiastically.

'Didn't hear a thing,' said Ethan.

I leaned forward. 'Enough's enough. We need an expert to help us – find out what's really going on.'

Being psychology students, we'd learned about parapsychology in class and knew there were societies who looked into paranormal activity. So I rang a well-known organisation, explained what had happened, and arranged for an investigator to visit us.

By now, we were taking it in turns to sleep in each other's rooms all together.

It was a rainy Thursday and I was home alone when I answered the door to a man with a frill of white hair around his ears. He wore round glasses, a grey checked suit and a wide, blue-striped tie.

'I'm Mr Hickmott, the lead investigator,' he said. 'I hear you have some possible poltergeist activity?'

I showed him into the lounge and watched in surprise as his eyes darted around the room. He was nervous! 'Has he sensed something scary?' I thought. 'What's the point of a jittery paranormal investigator?'

Over a cup of tea, I filled him in on the events. 'Most of the activity is in my room,' I said, standing up. 'Shall we?'

'Oh no,' he said, a bit too quickly. 'I'll take a look at the rest of the house first.' He leaned down to finger the antique fire tools, then followed me into the kitchen. 'There's the pressure cooker I told you about,' I said.

He grasped the lid, lifted it off, peered inside the vessel, then replaced the top carefully. 'Seems fine,' he said.

I wasn't impressed. 'What did you expect, streams of ectoplasm coming out of it?' I wanted to say.

After poking his head into the front room, he was finally ready to venture upstairs.

He hesitated before following me into my room and I resisted the temptation to roll my eyes.

With my desk in between us, I outlined what I'd witnessed in here. On the desk was a large, framed picture of me with my family, leaning backwards slightly on its stand as photo frames do.

'It's my belief,' he said, removing his specs, cleaning the lenses on a wedge of tissues he produced from his pocket, then plonking them back on his nose, 'that your so-called poltergeist activity is nothing more than rumblings produced by the underground trains that are probably running late into the night under the house, causing some movement. This is the East End of London and there are many tunnels here. I'll check and get back to you.'

'I don't think that's it,' I replied. 'We wondered the same thing, so me and Tarak – one of my flatmates – had a look at the map and we couldn't see one.'

'Well, as an expert–' he began, then our eyes were drawn to a movement on the desk. The heavy photo frame shuddered for a few seconds. Then it rose up slightly by a few millimetres, gently dropped back to its former position and finished by falling forward and landing face down on the desk with a smack.

Mr Hickmott's mouth dropped open and he gave a low,

strangled squeak. His eyebrows lifted so high they were visible above his spectacle frames, then he turned and ran down the stairs and out of the house incredibly nimbly for a man in his 50s.

'Will we hear from you?' I called after him, but he didn't reply.

'He knew something was here and he was frightened,' I told the others later. 'Hence his swift exit.'

Rosie clapped her hands together, startling us. 'If this place is too scary for a professional paranormal investigator, why the hell are we still here?'

'Too right,' agreed Ethan. 'Let's give Mrs Hocus Pocus our notice tomorrow. I'm done.'

All together, we only stayed in that house a few months and you can imagine how relieved the four of us were to find new digs. It was May by now, and we got a temporary place till the summer.

'Hurray!' said Rosie. 'A fresh house, free from spooks, just in time for us to get down to some serious study for our end-of-year exams.'

My friend Padma was staying with us and, while we all studied in separate rooms, we'd get together every few hours for a coffee break. The night before the final exam, it was 8pm and my turn to make coffee. I went to a couple of the rooms.

'Cups, please, if you want a drink, then I'll see you in the kitchen in 10 minutes!' I shouted as I walked through the house. I took Ethan's cup, then Rosie's and popped back to my attic room for my own cup. Padma and Tarak came up with theirs and I remember, I was stood in the middle of the room holding three empty coffee mugs. Then, all of a sudden the cups exploded – there's no other word for it – in my hand. They blew up, bits flying all over the room, as though each had a mini stick of dynamite in it, and I was left holding three handles with no cup attached. I couldn't believe it.

Me, Tarak and Padma looked at each other in stunned silence. Then Tarak said, 'Hey. Something hit me.' Reaching down, he pulled a brown chunk of one of the cups out of his trainer and held it out to us in the palm of his hand. 'This is some weird shit,' he breathed.

'No no no no *no*,' I wailed. 'I thought we'd left all this behind...'

'Those cups didn't just crack and fall to the ground,' observed Padma, who was a physics student. 'It was a proper explode-all-over-the-room situation, and there's no scientific explanation for that.'

Luckily, we were only there a few weeks and nothing else kooky occurred. Nor did it in the house we rented for our final year.

Looking back, it probably sounds like I'm telling fibs but I'm an honest person and I never took any kind of drugs as a student. What I've told you really happened.

But with such events, my first thought isn't, 'It's supernatural'. I took science at school and would look for objective reasons for things, not supernatural ones. Yet I experienced these episodes that there is no rational explanation for.

I've had eerie experiences since then. For example, I've seen balls of light on a couple of occasions – when my son was born and also when my father-in-law died – and I discovered that they're called orbs and are supposedly connected to the spirit world. And on holiday once with friends, a glass exploded in the same way the cups did in my student digs.

What are my theories? I think the scientific community are arrogant when they say that if something hasn't been scientifically verified, then it's not true, it's not real. I don't subscribe to that view anymore. I believe that we don't know everything, and mankind shouldn't be so pompous, because there's a whole big universe out there and we don't have all the answers. There are so many things we really don't have a clue about and can't explain.

THREE

BONDED BY BLOOD

Maria is a witch. Did her powers raise the dead – and solve the mystery of her friend's poltergeist?

I'VE BEEN A SENSITIVE since I was a girl and to me, the easiest way to describe how I am and that makes most sense to me is that I was born a witch. I believe I have a gift handed down through my family. I grew up knowing things, knowing there is more to the world than what's in front of you, but I don't believe anything unless I've experienced it personally, because I'm also trained in the field of medical science. Sounds contradictory, I know, but it works for me.

As it happens, I've been party to quite a few mystical phenomena over the years.

When I was five, I'd seen a film called *Troll* – an American comedy horror from the 1980s – that had really scared me. I got this idea the trolls would come and kidnap me, so had my bed positioned so I could see the door. Then at least then I'd be able to spot them as they came in and I could hide.

This night, Mum had put me to bed and I was lying there in the darkened room trying not to think about trolls. In the centre of the ceiling, my main light had a lampshade with figures of the Wombles all around it. I'd always been able to see well in the dark and now, a movement above me caught my eye. Glancing up at my Womble shade, on it was a face, life-size, a man's. Slim and sculpted with prominent cheekbones and a moustache, the face was topped with dark hair. And the mouth was moving, forming words as though the man were speaking quite normally.

'Am I imagining this?' I thought to myself. I was watching this man and I couldn't believe what I was seeing – I thought I must just be tired. Even so, the face stayed put and the lips kept moving. I wanted to hear what the man was saying but I couldn't, however hard I strained. I got the impression he was trying to get some point across to me but the longer I watched, the more frightened I became. After a few minutes, I sprang out of bed and ran into my mum's room.

Mum was asleep and I shook her shoulder as hard as I could.

'Mum, the man!' I cried. 'His face is on my lampshade

and he's talking to me!'

Mum opened her eyes reluctantly. 'You and your imagination,' she said, yawning and turning over. 'There's no man there. Go back to bed.'

'But Mum!' I said, impatient now, slapping the top of her back. 'He *is* there! He has black hair and a moustache and a thin face. Come and look!'

Mum turned back to stare at me, a perplexed expression on her face. She sat up and, pulling me onto the bed, she tugged open the top drawer of her bedside cabinet, drew out a photo in a large glass frame with red and pink hearts on it and put it in my hands.

'Is this him?' she asked.

It was a photo of my talking man. It wasn't like I'd seen an animated version of the picture – this chap looked slightly different, younger maybe, but it was definitely the face on my lampshade.

'How did you know?' I exclaimed. 'Who is it?'

Tears brimmed in her eyes. 'Your dad,' she said quietly. 'You know he died unexpectedly just before Christmas when you were one?'

This was the first picture I'd seen of him. Mum didn't give me all of this information then as I was too little, but as I got older, I pieced the story together.

She and my dad were very much in love, but they were

young and it had never occurred to her that she might lose him. After he'd died of a heart attack, her life fell apart and as the years went by, she found it tough being around me at times because apparently I'm very like him in looks and temperament. I do understand that, as his death was a hell of a shock for her. I'm sorry to report that she drowned her misery with alcohol and became a big drinker. So she'd kept Dad's picture hidden initially because it reminded her of that incredibly difficult time after he'd gone.

Having seen Dad in my room, it made me wonder what he wanted – maybe he had a vital message for me? I stayed with Mum that night and he never came to me again. So I never did find out what it was. I have to assume if it was that important, he'd have returned.

My Aunt Carol, who was my dad's sister, was the other witch in my family – very sadly, she passed away in 2005. Mum tried to keep that side of Carol's life away from me as it dismayed her, but I heard Aunt Carol used to hold seances and gatherings with other wise women.

Aunt Carol could sense my gifts. Once she took me upstairs, away from Mum, and slipped me a deck of tarot cards.

As an adult, I feel Aunt Carol around me. She comes to me in dreams and I used to see her face superimposed on those of certain older people, male and female. They'd suddenly wink at me in exactly the same way she would, even if winking was quite out of character for them.

By the time I was 10, I was aware I was a witch, although I hid it from my mum. I started learning about candle magic and herbal medicine from books in secret and stashed all my magic stuff under my bed.

I worked hard and my sensitivity grew. And after school when I was 12, Mum had some painful news for me.

'Maria love, your hamster Claws has died,' she told me. In the kitchen, Claws was on the table in a box. I touched his nose. It was dry and cold.

'Mum, get me my special pyjamas from the suitcase on your wardrobe,' I said. 'The tartan ones.'

'Can't imagine how you knew I'd put them there,' said Mum under her breath as she left the room.

Taking the pyjamas off her, I wrapped Claws in them and sat in an armchair by the log fire with him in my lap. I had a strong feeling I could bring him back to life. So I stroked his paws and rubbed his body and after a few minutes, Claws's eyes opened. He was back with us.

Mum was incredulous. 'Oh my God!' she said. 'Claws was dead and look at him now!' It was just one of those things – you can't explain it. I just knew I could do it.

What happened with my dad and Claws were interesting. But this event I'm going to relate now is what truly convinced me there is definitely something supernatural out there, even though we don't fully know what it is.

I was 16. Me and my friend Nasrin were at her house watching a Monty Python film one afternoon and discussing our dreams when we became aware of a gentle rattling sound.

'Where's that coming from?' asked Nasrin. 'It's a bit annoying.'

'Roadworks, maybe?' I said. 'Or heavy traffic?' We stuck our heads out of the window and looked up and down the street. All was quiet outside but the clattering continued.

'Maria,' said Nasrin, 'is it me, or is the floor vibrating?'

'It's like a train's passing, but we're not near a train line,' I said. 'Let's ignore it and return to the film.'

The room was a large one, with several big pieces of furniture. We'd been on the sofa and, leading the way back to it, I sat down first.

The noise got a little louder. It became clear it was coming from inside the room and we both turned towards it. To the right in the corner was a heavy sideboard with glass panels and it was rocking gently, ever so slightly, on its feet. By the window opposite, Nasrin gasped. 'Th-th-that's just not possible,' she stammered.

'Hmm,' I replied. 'There has to be a logical reason for

it.' As we watched, the sideboard speeded up until it was rocking crazily from side to side on its curved legs, the ornaments inside it tinkling as they slid back and forth across the shelves and crashed into each other.

Nasrin began crying. 'Come and sit here,' I said. As she took two steps in my direction, I felt a punch of freezing cold air through my back from the sofa, which went into my chest and head. It was horrible, but I closed my eyes, clenched my fists and puffed myself up like a bulldog, saying to myself, 'I'm not having this. I'M NOT HAVING THIS.'

Seeing me jerk my head back violently, Nasrin let out a scream. 'Your face has gone whitish grey!' she sobbed, shrinking back.

'Look, it's nothing,' I said, although that wasn't how I felt. 'If we pretend it's not happening, hopefully this will stop. Sit with me.'

She fell down next to me. As soon as her bottom hit the cushions, the sofa began to hop up and down, making small jumps from side to side. It was like something out of a Disney cartoon. That finished me off. By now we were both crying and screaming, so we leaped off the sofa, ran upstairs to her room and slammed the door.

Holding hands, we slowed our breathing and tried to calm ourselves. Us leaving the room seemed to have stopped the activity downstairs.

'Could it have been an earthquake?' asked Nasrin, blowing her nose.

'Only the sofa and cabinet were moving, though,' I said. 'The TV, coffee table and chairs were completely still. I doubt there are earthquakes that are selective like that.'

She'd lived in this house for six years, I'd visited loads of times and nothing like this had ever happened before. Her parents were charming and it was a very loving house – no negativity at all. I'd been into my witchy stuff for a few years but had always practised on my own with no ill effects... Then it came into my mind that Nasrin had done something to set this off.

'Nasrin,' I began carefully, 'have you done anything of late that could be described as – well, occult, that might have stirred up bad energy?'

'I – I did a blood bond with Phoebe at school two weeks ago,' she said, dabbing her eyes. 'Does that count?'

I folded my arms and fixed her with a look. Phoebe was notorious for her toxic, manipulative personality. But she was popular, and Nasrin had let Phoebe pressurise her into making a 'blood bond', whereby you each cut your finger, rub the wounds together and mix your blood, to bond you. Nasrin wanted to be part of Phoebe's in-crowd.

A film had recently come out about teenage witches and

it had created a whole load of witchy wannabees. But I'd been observing these girls and of course, without guidance they didn't know what they were doing. Even at 16, I was aware that making something as powerful as a blood bond with someone you don't trust is asking for trouble.

The girls had no clue how to protect themselves or approach the craft in a measured way.

'Well,' I sighed, 'that will be it. Making that blood bond with Phoebe most likely triggered this.'

We waited upstairs for Nasrin's parents to come home. I left and never went round again, although I stayed mates with her.

After that harrowing day, Nasrin told me the activity in her home wouldn't stop. Problems were constant. Objects moved on their own; for example, a clock flew off the wall towards her dad. Another time her mum had just put a stack of plates in the cupboard when the door burst open and the plates skimmed out one by one. Things would swoop into the air or slide off surfaces to land with a crash on the floor. The family tolerated it for a month and then moved out.

As I said, it was this event that really opened my eyes. I never expected the mystical world to manifest in such a physical way. It was terrifying. I do wonder if what Nasrin did kicked something into action in that house that was already unsettled but had been lying low.

I believe everyone is born with the capacity to tune into their psychic abilities and intuition. But we don't nurture it. Children can see things and feel things – I could. And when we start school, we have our inborn intuition programmed out of us and we lose that link to our subconscious.

I'm a dentist now and since I began my dental training, my creative side has diminished significantly. I'm having to replenish it and reopen my spiritual channels. I've had many supernatural experiences and it seems like a natural progression for me to learn how to hear spirits. For some reason, I can see them and feel them but not hear them, like with my dad on the lampshade. Not yet, anyway.

My journey of self-discovery and self-development is ongoing. Just call me the witchy, wise-woman dentist!

FOUR

ROOM 18

Who wouldn't want to spend a night in a fabulous castle for free? Not Vivian, after her last experience within its walls...

I WANT TO STATE this plainly: I don't believe in ghosts or the supernatural. Nevertheless, the event I'm going to relate happened to me and my husband recently; make of it what you will.

Giles and I are both garden designers and we had an appointment with a client at her cottage to survey the site and make preliminary sketches. It was in the Welsh countryside, so we decided to treat ourselves to a night's stay at a magnificent castle I'd found nearby.

Our break started out well enough. After taking measurements and plenty of photos of the client's garden, we drove the few miles to our hotel.

'Wow!' I said as we swept around a corner and the fairy tale castle, with its speckled, pewter stone facade, rose up before us. 'Turrets, arched mullioned windows – the lot.

Great choice by me!'

Parking the car, we grabbed our bags and tramped up the stone steps to the entrance. 'I can imagine you as a damsel in distress, my love, and me riding in on my white steed, resplendent in my armour, to assist you,' joked Giles, making jabs with an imaginary sword.

'Knowing how clumsy you are, you'd fall off your horse and it would be me rescuing you!' I laughed.

Pushing open the heavy door, we marvelled at the scarlet walls above the carved, dark wood panelling running the length of the hall, lending the place a warm, intimate feel despite the high ceilings. 'I guess I shouldn't be surprised this is huge inside, but the reception desk is so far away that I might expire before we reach it!' whispered Giles, making as if to flop onto one of several leather Chesterfields that lined the hallway.

'No you don't,' I said, grabbing his sleeve playfully. 'I want food – let's get to our suite pronto!'

A young man showed us to our room, which was incredible – but more on that later. We unpacked, had dinner and prepared to go to bed. That's when the problems began.

Giles and I were so unsettled by our experience that I emailed a complaint to the manager a few days after we got home. Here's what I wrote.

Dear Sir,

My husband and I have just arrived home from a stay in your property, and to be honest, we passed a pretty dreadful night there. We hadn't read anything about the castle beforehand and were thrilled to be checked into Room 18 which, as you know, is sumptuous, with its four-poster bed and antique mahogany furniture.

After an excellent dinner in your restaurant, I went up to bed, while my husband took himself off to one of your office rooms to work on the plans for our new project. Our bedroom was large, the door several feet away from the end of the bed. I'd brought my own dressing gown with me, a silky peach garment, which hung on the door's brass hook with its back towards me.

By 11pm, I was propped up on pillows listening to a podcast on my phone as I do most nights to unwind, facing the door. I'd turned the side lamp down and was relaxing, enjoying the warm yellow glow it cast on that part of the room. The rest was in semi-darkness. My earphones were in, fingers laced across my belly, and I was gazing up at the ceiling as I focused on the podcast presenter's voice when a movement opposite caused me to lower my eyes. My dressing gown was swinging a little on its hook and rippling to the left, as though caught in a breath of wind from the side.

There was a gap under the door where a sliver of light seeped in from the hall. 'There must be a draught coming up from the door,' I thought. The dressing gown stilled and fell back into place so, shutting my eyes, I turned my attention back to my podcast. 'Actually,' I thought, 'wind under the door would blow it out at the bottom, surely, rather than from the side?'

As I was pondering this, I heard a gentle swish ahead of me. My eyes sprang open.

My dressing gown was billowing out, bellying in the middle as though someone were pressing a hand into the centre of it from behind. As I watched in horror, the gown began to fill up with the shape of shoulders, then a back, then arms as though someone was slowly putting it on until it stood proud from the door. The pressure inside caused it to lift off the hook and it stood for a second before me, belt hanging down at the sides, its back taut as though someone were holding the front closed. Then it deflated and fell to the floor, crumpling into a pool of shimmering fabric.

Yanking out my earphones, my heart thudding, I started a text to my husband. Then I thought the better of it and shook my head. All that had happened was I hadn't hung the dressing gown up properly and the wind under the door had filled it up, then it had slipped to the ground.

Uneasy though I was, I drifted off to sleep, although I half-woke several times during the night. I heard Giles come to bed but was too shattered to start a conversation.

We were both silent at breakfast. In the car as we left, Giles said, 'So... how did you sleep last night?'

'Why do you ask?' I replied casually, shooting him a sideways look as I tinkered with the satnav.

'Because you seemed restless and I had quite a freaky experience in the room,' he replied, frowning as he drove.

'You tell me your story first,' I said.

'Well... I got into bed around 2am and lay awake for a while, ideas for designs running through my head. Then I gradually became aware of the oddest feeling – that there was someone else in the room with us. And this I really can't account for – I got the definite impression that this someone wasn't human.

'Also,' he continued, 'it was difficult to get into the room – your dressing gown was blocking the door when I tried to open it. You could have hung it back up, knowing I was due to come in!'

I described what I'd seen. I hadn't wanted to touch my dressing gown after that and had picked it up in a towel and stowed it in the bin before we left the room that morning.

'Sorry, Viv, but I'm certain there was no draught coming

from under the bedroom door,' said Giles. 'Yes, this is an ancient castle, but it was still and silent when I came up, without a breath of wind in the corridor.

'Look for the place online and see what comes up,' he said with a nervous laugh. 'Maybe it's haunted.'

I did, and then Giles and I were in shock. This is your hotel and you must be aware what people are writing about it.

'This castle has a reputation for ghostly goings-on,' I read out, 'and is a favourite haunt, pardon the pun, for those seeking supernatural experiences. Room 18 in particular has generated several reports of paranormal activity.'

I am, in fact, quite upset that we were put in a room with so many ghostly tales attached to it. While Giles and I still don't believe in apparitions, it's true that the energy in that room is, shall I say, poisonous, and that the experience ruined my sleep for quite a few nights.

Yours,

Vivien Sky.

And the manager's reply:

Dear Mrs Sky,

Many thanks for your email. I'm sorry to hear about your

and Mr Sky's experiences in Room 18. While we do not advertise our hotel as one where guests may encounter the supernatural, as you say, we are aware that some have had certain things happen which they describe as otherworldly, but which added a welcome frisson to their stay. I will certainly heed your words and warn future guests that Room 18 may not be suitable if they have what might be termed an active imagination.

As compensation, I would like to offer you a free night, with dinner and Champagne, at the castle on the date of your choice. Naturally, your chamber will be situated some distance from Room 18.

Warmest wishes,

Mr K. Gunnett, Manager

Does it surprise you that Giles and I turned down Mr Gunnett's proposition?

FIVE

MUM'S THE WORD

For the last three decades, Aurora, a family doctor, has shared her home with a variety of spirits, from the mischievous to the malevolent. Here is her tale...

I'VE ALWAYS FELT I'M quite a psychically perceptive person, and this was confirmed when I moved into the three-bedroom house I currently live in 32 years ago with my then-husband. I first became aware there was supernatural activity here early on when I was in the living room – you could often hear footsteps in the bedroom above, which is my room, when there was no one upstairs.

I had my girls, Julie and Sara, in the early 1990s and when they were tiny, they were particularly sensitive to the uncanny events. One time, I was feeding Julie, my younger daughter, in the kitchen in her highchair. Suddenly, she looked up and started smiling and waving at something behind me.

'What is it, darling?' I asked, turning round. 'Lady!'

she giggled, pointing. But there was nothing there. This happened several times with both girls, but they weren't scared. It was fine by me, as long as they were happy. I asked them about the 'kitchen lady' when they were older, but they couldn't remember.

When the girls reached adolescence, the supernatural activity got worse, with more things happening, especially centred around the bathroom and Julie. Several times, she'd be in the bath and the door would fly open on its own. This she actually found really scary as, not surprisingly, she felt vulnerable in the bath.

Around this time, which was about 15 years ago, I came home from my shift at the surgery early, at 4pm. It was a summer's day and the girls, then teenagers, were out. As I approached the house, I could see steam wafting out of the bathroom window, which I'd left open. 'What's going on?' I thought.

Divorced by now, I had a good friend, Jay, and he was fond of hiding in the house and bushes and jumping out to frighten me. I considered this very childish, as we were in our 40s, but he thought it was hilarious. So I assumed the bathroom steam must be down to him.

Opening the front door, I could hear the sound of rushing water, very loud, in the bathroom upstairs. 'Jay?' I shouted. 'Are you there? Hey, this isn't funny – you're really scaring me. Come out!'

Feeling frightened, I didn't want to go upstairs to see what was going on. There was a negative, chilling atmosphere in the house, despite the warm weather. I'd been the last person to leave that morning and I definitely hadn't left the taps on. Slowly, on tiptoe, I went up the stairs, calling, 'Jay? Come on now – that's enough.' Reaching the bathroom, I poked my nose in through the open door. Both bath taps were on full, scalding water coming out of one and causing the steam I'd seen outside. The water was draining away down the plughole. Leaning forward, I turned the taps off and, with my heart in my mouth, I checked the bedrooms carefully in turn.

The house was empty apart from me.

'Could it have been an intruder – a stranger?' I thought. 'But then how likely is it that they'd try to run themselves a bath? And how did they get in – and out? The doors were locked.' I later found out that Jay had been at work all day. It wasn't his doing.

After that, the taps in the sink and bath would turn themselves on every now and then – they still do. Not as forcefully as that time, but when there's no one around to operate them.

There is still quite a bit of activity in the house. Often while I'm sitting in the living room on the sofa, like I am now, talking to you on the phone, the door will open itself. It has a handle, and almost every evening, while I'm watching TV, you can actually see the handle go down as the door is pushed open. It does make me jump. A lot goes on in the kitchen; items will roll off the surfaces on to the floor. There's a large picture of a horse on the wall in the kitchen. Occasionally it decides to jump off the wall on its own, which frightened the life out of a friend of mine, Ava, the other afternoon.

We were having coffee in the kitchen when the picture kind of leaped to the floor – it didn't simply drop down, as it might have done if the hook had broken. It's big, and there was such a bang as it hit the tiles. We both saw it happen and started at the noise.

'How did that happen?' Ava asked, shuddering. 'There's nobody else here and we're nowhere near it.'

I put an arm around her and laughed. 'It's only the ghosts,' I said. 'It's nothing to be frightened of. They're naughty, but not malicious. They just want you to know they're here – they're saying hello.'

Though these aren't major things, they all add up. The ghosts often hide objects – maybe they think it's funny. The things that have disappeared in this house, and eventually emerge from somewhere completely different months, sometimes even years, later.

For example, we gave one of our girls a silver bracelet for her 21st birthday. She loved it, and left it by her bed that night, on the bedside table. It wasn't there the next day and we looked high and low for it – nothing. Then it turned up six years later, in a cupboard in my bedroom.

And – this is really peculiar – the house ghosts seem to love teaspoons. You know how we all lose the odd teaspoon? About five years ago, my teaspoons began to disappear one by one from the cutlery drawer. I'd buy another set of six, and they'd vanish too. I was down to two teaspoons, then one day I opened the drawer and there were 10 spoons. After that, every day, there would be one or two more in there. Now they vanish regularly, then some will turn up in the drawer. I counted them the other day – there were about 23.

Another interesting thing has concerned the animals in this house – they've sometimes reacted badly to the ghosts. I've had several cats over the years. For example, our cat Sidney was sensitive to our paranormal guests. Sidney would be on the sofa with us in the evening, then he'd sit up straight and you'd see him scanning the room, as though his eyes were following something tall that was walking across the floor.

Once we were looking after my friend's Alsatian, King, for a few days and something terribly creepy happened.

King was a huge, friendly dog. The first night he was here, he was in the lounge with Sara and me as we watched TV. All of a sudden King stiffened, sat up, bared his teeth and started growling. Just like the cat, you saw his head move as though he was watching something the height of a person walk across the room. He was so agitated that it really scared me and my daughter, although he was fine the next two evenings. That was five years ago.

As well as the bathroom taps incident and King's reaction, there was another event that unnerved me involving Sara's cat, Jaguar. This was three years ago and, after that, I decided to take action on the house spirits.

Sara brought Jaguar here at Easter and the cat stayed on to live with me.

Jaguar would happily trot up and down the stairs, and she loved to snooze on my bed. One morning, I came down and let her in from the garden. She ran to the stairs as if to trot up to my bed as usual, then she stopped dead at the bottom step. Glaring at the top of the stairs, she arched her back, hissed, then fled from the house. After that, she refused to go upstairs; when I lifted her to carry her up, she'd fight in my arms, so I'd put her down again. I'd been getting the unsettling feeling that somehow, something had changed in the house and Jaguar's behaviour confirmed it.

I had a new partner, Liam, who was very psychically aware and could sense the presences in the house. I hadn't told Liam about the incident with Jaguar, but soon after, he came down the stairs and said out of the blue, 'I'm sorry to tell you this, but the reason the paranormal activity is centred around the bathroom is that someone hanged themselves in there.'

I was speechless, but I had heard some of the history of the house. I know that, very sadly, the couple that lived here before me had a child who died at the age of six. I don't know any details.

A few days later when Liam was over, he turned to me with a strange, distant look in his eyes and said, 'I can see four people in this house – including your mum – but there's also a fifth one who doesn't belong here. Your mum keeps the other three in check, but she can't control this fifth one, although she tries to.'

I was astonished – and upset. He knew my mum had passed on, but it was news to me that it was *her* that was haunting me. You see, I've been told several times that I have four guardian spirits and that one is my mum. I was first told this by a medium many years ago, when I was quite young, before I had my babies. 'When you have children,' he said, 'you don't ever have to worry about them because your mum will be looking out for them.'

Mum died in 1990, a few years before my first girl was born. I'd been very close to her – I didn't have much of a relationship with my dad. So it makes sense that it would be Mum who'd be looking after me. I have no idea who the other three are. Maybe they're relatives as well. But what about this fifth one? Where had they come from and why?

I had no way of knowing, but I decided something had to be done about this negative, uncontrollable spirit. I found out you could do a 'psychic clearing' of the house using sage and candles, known as smudging. 'Worth a try,' said Liam, with a shrug.

I bought a white sage stick online and, one afternoon, Liam and I lit a candle in each room, including the bathroom. Lighting the sage from the living room candle, we walked around the house, wafting sage smoke into the corner of every room and cupboard. As we walked, I repeated, 'Leave this house. You are not welcome. LEAVE! YOU ARE NOT WELCOME!'

'Go back to wherever you came from!' Liam said over and over, beside me.

And it seemed to work. After that, Jaguar was happy to go upstairs again and the place felt peaceful.

I don't know what that was about. I believe a spirit had invited itself in, and it was a malevolent one. And the clearing got rid of it. But the others are still here – they often wake me up at night, daily almost. They'll open the bedroom door, or I sense people in my room. I find it comforting, especially since I'm convinced one is Mum.

Of course, it's possible that other entities come and go. Maybe the child who died, her grieving parents, the distressed person who killed themselves in the bathroom – who knows. But I don't feel that negative presence here anymore, the one that upset Jaguar, so I'm not worried.

Oh, I nearly forgot. A friend of mine left a video camera running in the living room one night. When we watched the playback next day, most of it was tedious. But at one point, we spotted a light orb moving from the door across the floor. I've heard that spirits often appear as lights. I think that was a cat spirit, because it was close to the ground.

I have a huge garden with a large, circular flowerbed in the middle. Years ago, I spotted one of my cats suddenly start chasing round and round the flowerbed, as though it was playing with another cat. Then it changed direction and began running the other way. So I reckon there are spirit cats about the place.

I must tell you that, as we've been speaking, the house ghosts are letting me know they're aware we're talking about them. I've just gone into the kitchen with the phone and the cutlery drawer is wide open...

SIX

COLD COMFORT

*Harry, a maths teacher, contacted me about
an incident from his student days...*

THIS HAPPENED WHEN I was at university a decade ago.
I lived with the same couple of guys, Tom and Isaac, from
the first year through to the third year. I got to know them
well and they're still great mates of mine today.

In our last year, we had to find a new house a few
months into the first term due to problems with the
landlord. So in the January, we took another house that
was a bit tatty. Isaac had the front room downstairs as his
bedroom and there was always a weird, oppressive feeling
in there – you'd shiver whenever you went in.

It was winter and, as Isaac had the best TV, I remember
sitting up with him in there one night watching the
Superbowl, which would start late and be on till 3am. All
the rooms had heating, but his had cold areas that were
freezing and nothing you could do would warm them up

– the centre of the room was particularly bad, like it had an ice pocket there. We couldn't understand it. And we were so chilly that night, even after knocking back a load of beers, with the radiator blasting out heat and blankets wrapped around our bodies.

A couple of nights later, the three of us went into town to the pub. Tom had a few too many drinks, got into an argument with one of the locals and booted the guy's car, putting a dent in it. Unfortunately for Tom, the car owner was a karate black belt and he gave Tom quite a beating.

We took our battered pal to the hospital and called the police as well. Two days later, a policeman dropped in at the house to take our statements. We weren't expecting the copper so, as we had a bit of dope in the house, we were in a panic hoping we hadn't left some out somewhere.

Me, Tom and Isaac were in the lounge with the policeman and he kept glancing around the room as we talked. We were worried – had he smelled something?

As the copper was about to leave, he stopped on the doorstep and, gesturing towards Isaac's room, said, 'Can I just have a look in there?'

'Yeah,' said Isaac, praying all was as it should be in his room, as were we.

The copper walked into the room and looked around, with us behind him. Then he said, 'I thought I'd been here before.'

And we were like, 'What do you mean?'

'There was a hanging,' he said. 'Someone hanged themselves from the light fitting in the centre of this room.' He pointed up at it. 'A student from your university. He died. I can't tell you any details, obviously, but it was a couple of years ago. I attended the scene. And I see all his furniture is still here – same bed, same wardrobe, same desk.'

I said, 'No... Are you sure it was here?'

He was quite certain.

The man left, and I turned to Isaac and Tom. 'Well, that figures. That dreadful cold spot in the centre of the room is under the light fitting. That poor guy breathed his last in your room, Isaac. Imagine how sad, how utterly desperate he must have felt to do that.'

Isaac went in, grabbed his quilt and came out. 'I'm never sleeping in there again,' he shuddered. 'I'm on the lounge sofa from now on.'

That was February and we stayed in the house till the end of June. The sofa was lumpy, but there was no way Isaac was going back to that bedroom. I felt fine as my room was upstairs and I'm a pretty sceptical person, but once Isaac had taken his stuff out, we locked that room up for the rest of our time there. Just in case.

SEVEN

VICTOR VICTORIOUS

As a teenager, Petra fell madly in love – with a building.
Her association with it was to bring her a string of startling
experiences over the years...

EVERY DAY ON MY way to school in a busy part of
London, I would pass a huge office block with several
floors. It was a magnificent building, with Greek-style
columns running up the front. Peering in through the
window on tiptoe, I could make out an ornate tiled
entrance hall with a wonderful mosaic floor.

My story really begins when, as an adult, I got a job with
the local council and, astonishingly, found myself based
at offices within the building. I was fascinated by it and
undertook research into the architect who built it, Victor.
I discovered that he had been commissioned to build this
edifice as the headquarters of a company in the 1900s. It
took two years to erect, and Victor continued to enlarge
the building over the course of 20 years.

Part of my job was to take care of the building. I believe Victor understood my devotion to his creation and that he, in turn, took care of me.

There was very much an air of the supernatural about the place, a topic that interested me greatly.

Late in the day, I would often hear footsteps on the floor above while I was there with only one security guard, who was sitting opposite me. On another occasion, I was talking about Victor to a new member of staff as he was stacking binders in a bookcase. When he'd finished, within minutes, they all flew out and landed in a heap on the floor.

Lights would regularly turn themselves on and off. The switches had actually been flicked down – you would have to go over and flick them up again. It wasn't just a case of the light tubes popping.

I also escaped unscathed from several bad electric shocks, a robbery attempt, a light fitting falling on my head, two collapsed ceilings and a couple of fires within the building. All courtesy of my guardian angel Victor, I believe.

Some days, the sound of wheels turning could be heard in the basement, and workmen regularly said they didn't want to go down there as they felt someone was watching them. An architect refused to return after I argued with him about his unsympathetic plans for refurbishment. We were on the second floor, and while we were rowing, a hefty oak door behind us slammed shut by itself – and it had been propped open with a heavy weight. I've never seen someone run down the stairs so fast! Needless to say, his plans were never carried out. I suspect Victor disliked the man's ideas as much as I did.

The most frightening thing that happened to me was on a staircase.

I was walking down a steep flight of stairs from the third floor carrying a heavy box so big I couldn't see over it. At the bottom of the short flight was a large, open window. Starting down the stairs, I slipped on the first step and felt myself start to pitch forward. Suddenly I was pulled back by the shoulders and, luckily, I found my footing.

'My goodness,' I puffed, putting down the box and turning around. 'Thank you – that would have been a nasty fall!' I looked up and down the corridor – it was completely empty and silent. There were no doors nearby that someone could have slipped through. And no one could have passed me on the stairs without me seeing them. Perplexed, I murmured a silent prayer of gratitude. Whoever had grabbed me had definitely saved my life.

One of the new security guards had a strange experience. He had heard the stories about Victor and mentioned he'd love to 'see' him, but quickly added that he didn't believe in ghosts or suchlike.

A few days later, he had a tale for me.

'I arrived early one morning,' he said, 'and was walking through the office to open the back door for the builders who were working on a job when I noticed someone sitting at a desk, quite a way from me. It was a man, dressed smartly in a high-collared white shirt and a suit.

'I'd just unlocked the doors, so I knew I was the only person in the building at the time. The light was dim, so I turned to switch another one on and, when I turned back, the desk was empty.

'Before this, I was a total sceptic where ghosts are concerned, but I do wonder if this meant your Victor wasn't happy with those particular builders.'

Other staff told me they would often smell the overpowering odour of old-fashioned, sweet tobacco, although I never had that experience. This was a non-smoking building, but I know Victor smoked a pipe, so for decades, he must have been puffing away while he strolled around the place.

Eventually, I decided I wanted to know more about Victor personally, so I ordered a rare out-of-print book about his architecture. To my delight, it had a picture of Victor in it – this was the first time I'd seen what he looked like. Distinguished with upright bearing, he had an aquiline nose, centred-parted hair and a neat beard. Sporting a natty spotted bow tie, the corner of a folded handkerchief poked out of his jacket breast pocket.

I was astonished because I felt certain this was the man I'd noticed on several occasions outside the building, often accompanied by a chap in an antiquated railway worker's uniform. Strangely, some weeks after, I was arriving for a meeting about the building miles away, only to see them walking across the road together! The Victor figure looked almost otherworldly, with bright blue eyes and glowing white hair. This time, I was determined to approach the man and ask who he was. However, just as I caught up with them, the pair literally disappeared in front of me. I never saw Victor again.

I had to find out more about my architect, and a bit more digging revealed that he and his family had lived in a large house in London, but also owned a country cottage not far from the sea, where he loved to spend time with his wife and children and his wide circle of friends.

Built around 1875, Victor added to and extended the house over a period of several years. One of his children, his daughter Elise, spent a lot of time there with the family nanny. Elise suffered from ill health most of her short life, dying in her late teens, and it was thought that the sea air would be beneficial for her. She was said to adore the house and I hoped that, if I went there, I would be able to pick up signs of her spirit.

I was very excited at the idea of going to Victor's former home, somewhere that had been so special to him and his loved ones, where they had slept, ate and laughed together.

I was to have a couple of unnerving, time-slip experiences there.

Arriving on an overcast, early spring day, I approached the yellow brick farmhouse and rapped on the door with the brass knocker. A cheerful woman with chestnut hair pulled into a ponytail let me in. Walking through the front door was amazing – it felt like coming home. The architectural style was so obviously Victor. He loved arches, wood panelling and cupboards – if there was a spare wall where he could stick a cupboard, he would! He built this house shortly before the block I worked in and it reminded me of a miniature, toned-down version of it. So many elements were the same – balustrades, panelling, arches, fireplaces and windows. I strolled around the ground floor – the building had a warm feeling, cosy despite its large size.

In the living room, as the house's owner and I chatted about my journey, the temperature suddenly dropped by several degrees. Feeling a chill behind me, I knew Victor was there and shivered.

'Is everything OK?' asked the woman.

'Yes,' I replied, 'but is it all right if I nip upstairs and look in the bedrooms?'

I didn't need to ask for a sign that Victor was around but, climbing the stairs, I wanted to get more of a sense of Elise. I wandered around the first floor, listening carefully. Hearing a rattle coming from one room, I popped my head around the door. Was this Elise? I needed another sign. I left the room and called, 'Elise?' Again, I heard the rattle, coming from the same room.

Going back in, I stood at the window and suddenly saw what Elise would have seen, a wonderful view of the garden, but different to the one I'd just walked past on the way in – this was a fleeting vision from a distant century. Then it was gone and I was back to the present day, gazing over the garden as it currently is.

Elise loved this house and I knew she was very happy here, which pleased Victor immensely.

The house's owner met me at the bottom of the stairs. 'Love, you're crying,' she said gently, touching my arm. Tears were streaming down my face. I was so full of emotion I could hardly speak. She led me back to the lounge, where she'd made a pot of tea.

We sat down. 'I felt very drawn to this house,' she

explained. 'When we came to view it, it had such a joyful atmosphere and I knew me and my family would be content here. And we are.

'Once or twice, I thought I heard children's laughter in the garden, but it was empty,' she continued. 'I believe previous occupants have said the same. No one has seen anything though, as far as I know.'

Sipping my hot tea, nodding as I listened to her words, something odd happened. I became aware that her face was changing, from that of a 30-something modern woman to a much older lady, the scraped-back ponytail becoming a silver bun. The face of someone from another time was superimposed over hers for a few seconds before returning to normal. I got the distinct feeling that, many years ago, Victor had occupied the very spot I was sitting in, by the fireplace, looking at his wife framed by the French windows as he enjoyed the view of the garden, just as I was today.

It was a moving and fitting end to my quest to get to know the man who had designed my favourite building.

EIGHT

SHIPSHAPE

You might think you're safe from spooks out at sea on a ship full of sailors. But as Edgar found out, you'd be wrong...

I SPENT MORE THAN 25 years in the Navy, beginning on a large warship, an old vessel built in the 1960s. Age 23, I began as a mechanic and ended up as an officer leading my own department. Although I didn't see active service myself, over the decades that ship had been a backdrop to scores of war casualties and men losing their lives.

The events I'm going to describe happened during my first few years in the Navy on this ship. I became an electronics and radar engineer, also working on explosives, weapon systems and missile systems. My time was spent at sea, docked in a UK naval base or in foreign ports.

There were so many paranormal incidents. I'll just mention the main episodes.

On one occasion, I'd just started watch-keeping, which concerns overseeing the smooth running of the ship, and there were two people on watch at a time. We did this at night and Glen, the chap I was on watch with, kept playing jokes on me as we were doing our rounds. We'd each go into a compartment, check all the equipment, then meet for a chat. And these ships are huge. The other sailors were asleep, so the place was deserted.

I'd be walking along and Glen would jump out from behind a piece of equipment, just messing around. We were young, after all.

I got a bit tired of it, though. This particular evening, I'd nipped up the ladder to the bridge and I thought I'd get my own back on him. I could hear someone walking around on the deck I'd just left, so I hid around the corner by the top of the ladder.

Footsteps clanged up the ladder, rung by rung, and I thought, 'Right. I've got him!' As the steps reached the top, I sprang out and yelled, 'Boo!'

But no one was there. Not a soul.

A few weeks later, something happened that I found really difficult to handle.

Above the bridge, where the ladders were, there was a platform for the weapon systems. Dusk was falling and I'd gone up the ladder to the platform and made sure everything was locked up and secure. Then I went back down the ladder, strolled about 20 meters, and went up onto another platform to check that equipment. Then I noticed a movement on the platform I'd just left. Glancing over, I saw a figure. Thinking it was a friend of mine, I pelted down the ladder and back up to that platform to say hello – and it was deserted. But there's no way anybody could have got off without me seeing them.

You'd think that was the worst of it. But after I'd returned to the other platform to continue checking the equipment, I looked over to where I'd just come from. There was a dark shadow, a man's figure, just stood there. It was black, thick and dense, but I couldn't make out any detail. It was a huge shock. I ran back down the ladder and legged it to the mess to find some real, live human company.

After I'd started telling friends what I'd witnessed, people came forward to report having often seen apparitions in that area that would appear and disappear. I later heard that section of the ship was said to be really haunted.

The place where I did my main job, the bottom deck, stretched virtually the whole width of the part of the ship that was under the water. My mess area, where I lived and slept, was a couple of decks up from there. I'd be working down on the bottom deck very late: 11pm, 12am, 1am – all hours.

One night, doing the rounds on the bottom deck, I just knew – felt – there was something there with me.

We did these rounds every night. There were several doors. You would unlock one, go into the room, check the equipment, then lock the door behind you and move to the next. I'd done it so often that I knew the particular sound of each lock. This being such an old ship, it had big, long-handled door keys, like jailer's keys.

It was after midnight, gloomy below deck and musty with the tang of stale seawater. I'd just checked the apparatus in the last room, locked the door behind me and started walking away to get to my mess area. Then I heard sounds that made the short hairs on the back of my neck stand up. It was like an echo of myself, the movements I'd just made a few seconds earlier. The door slammed, the key turned in the lock – I recognised the sound of the last lock I'd operated – and footsteps started following me, the same weight and pace as my own. I tell you, I ran hard up through those decks and shut myself in my room, panting.

Lots of sailors were seeing things or having experiences they couldn't explain, but I didn't know this until I started speaking out about it. Keith, who used to work overnights in the gangway (a narrow walkway) told me his story.

'I was sat in a prefab cabin in the gangway having a cuppa with the door shut,' he said. 'A bang came on the roof, which was odd, as I don't know how someone could have reached it. Next came knocking on the door and sides of the cabin. You know what the lads are like for taking the mick, so I ignored it, hoping they'd go away. Then there was heavy thumping on the door, so hard the cabin was shaking. That riled me. 'Just piss off!' I shouted, jumping to my feet and kicking the door open to give whoever it was a shock. I stuck my head out – no one was there. I searched the area but found nothing.

'So I went back in to my tea. It was on a small wooden table with a flap at the side, and I sat myself down on the stool next to it. Minutes later, the flap shot up, spilling the tea everywhere.'

For me, the paranormal activity culminated in a particularly alarming episode. Thank goodness I wasn't alone for it.

I had a friend, Richard, who was a couple of ranks higher than me and a decade older. Night was falling and we were in his equipment room discussing the ghostly goings-on. At the top of the room was a vent, called a fan chamber, for the air conditioning, which came from the next room. Normally you weren't aware of its output, but suddenly it began belting out scalding hot air.

'What's going on there?' said Richard. 'Is something on fire?'

'There must be a problem of some sort,' I said. So we went to the room where the fan was. The heat had died down and everything looked fine, so we went back to the equipment room and took our seats. Minutes later, Richard said, 'Can you feel that? Like a throbbing in the air?'

In the corner was a lamp. Tiny movements led us both to turn our heads – the lamp had started vibrating on its table.

At first, we were frozen in our seats with surprise. The shudders and rattles got stronger and stronger, until the lamp was rocking on its base and shaking fit to explode. Next, there were violent bangs and thumps on the roof. The air from the vent began blowing icy cold.

I was speechless with shock, but after a few minutes of this, Richard began to shout. 'Look, whoever you are, I don't care. Do your worst! You're not frightening me away from this room. This is where I work!'

Unbelievably, the commotion stopped. The lamp was still, the roof was quiet and the air from the vent became unobtrusive, as usual. All was peaceful.

'Wow!' I said, limp with relief. 'That's told it!'

Richard never experienced anything else untoward up there again. It was as if by him saying that he's not worried, he's not going, he's not scared, that the spirit activity went away for good.

Plenty of other paranormal-type things have happened to me, but I try to dismiss them, put them out of my mind and move on. I feel I am sensitive to this stuff, but I'm not easily scared. I left the Navy some years ago and, since then, I've been on ghost hunts in a couple of supposedly very haunted locations and 'known' we wouldn't have any experiences because nothing was there.

I'm a technician, with a Master's degree in engineering, and I have some theories about supernatural experiences. It's said that we only perceive a small percentage of what's actually going on around us. For example, with the light spectrum, we only see a small part of it, and when it comes to our hearing, we can only hear within a limited frequency, for example dogs and bats can hear things we can't. Regarding energy, we can't see radar signals, electricity or radio signals. So as humans, we have quite a narrow bandwidth, or range that we're aware of. But I think some people have a wider bandwidth than others, and whether I like it or not, that seems to include me. I've seen shadow figures walk through walls in hotel rooms and discussed poltergeist activity I've witnessed in supermarket aisles with the owner.

Maybe I'll fill you in on the other stories some time... if you want to hear them.

NINE

DIFFERENT STROKES

Marjorie and Ted made light of their ghost at first – then things turned darker...

THERE WERE PLENTY OF paranormal events in the house I'm going to tell you about. Originally a shepherd's cottage, made of hefty grey local stone, it was built in the 1700s and extended over the following century. My husband Ted and me raised our four children there – two boys and two girls.

Situated in a remote area of the windswept Yorkshire Dales, we lived there for 20 years. It was a quirky house and, believe it or not, we had at least one ghost with us all that time.

On the first couple of occasions that we heard things, we thought, well, it's such an old place it's bound to have a few rattles and creaks. Then the sounds became quite definite – soft footsteps, all over the house. You'd hear whoever it was walking around – there would be footsteps in the room with you sometimes. We all heard them.

In the very beginning, Ted and me were alarmed but we loved the house and made light of things for the sake of the children. Then we got used to the noises and didn't even talk about them much. We were a calm, sensible family and accepted that the ghost was around. It didn't do us any harm and the kids decided it was a 'him', who they nicknamed Bertie. At one point, we had three dogs and they paid no attention to Bertie at all. Actually, there were occasions where you'd hear footsteps walk up to the dogs and stop, as though Bertie wanted to stroke them.

He'd move things sometimes – for example, a loo roll shot off the worksurface in the kitchen, and a necklace was picked up off the sideboard by an unseen hand, carried through the air and dropped at my feet.

None of us saw our ghost but my daughter Keely had a boyfriend called Colin who spotted someone we assume was Bertie.

Colin was sleeping over and nipped to the loo in the middle of the night. In the darkness, Colin saw a man on the landing, passing him on the way to the bathroom. The man had gone when Colin came out. Colin climbing back into bed woke Keely up.

'You didn't tell me someone else was staying,' he told her. 'I just saw a man outside our door.' Keely roared with laughter. 'There's only us here, so you must have met our ghost, Bertie. You're honoured – none of us have seen him!'

'You're nuts,' he retorted. 'I'm not spending time in a house with a ghost.' And he never came round again.

Soon after, Keely found out Colin had been cheating on her for months. We reckon Bertie knew Colin was going to hurt Keely and appeared to Colin to scare him away for her sake. Keely dumped Colin not long after his encounter with Bertie.

But there was one thing that happened in that house that was absolutely terrifying. And I wasn't the only person to witness it...

This particular night was a few years after Colin had met Bertie. My husband and the three older kids had gone to bed. I was sat in the lounge with my other daughter, Jess, who was 15 at the time, in front of a blazing fire talking about our day.

Suddenly a right commotion started up in the next room, bangs and crashes. 'What on earth?' I said to Jess. 'It sounds like one of the dogs is in there, destroying the room. That's not like them!'

Jess raised her eyebrows. 'Mum, two of the dogs are on the sofa and one's behind you. It's not them.' It was as though someone or something was throwing huge objects around the room that were landing heavily on the floor.

'There's got to be someone in there!' I said, clutching at her arm. 'It's obviously a burglar.'

The bangs and crashes got louder. The dogs were looking in the direction of the noise, but they didn't move or look fazed. 'Why aren't the dogs upset if there's an intruder in the house?' I said.

I jumped up and so did Jess. 'We have to do something,' she said urgently. 'Otherwise whoever it is will come for us next.'

With shaking hands, I grabbed the poker from by the fire and held it in front of me. We went out into the hall and in the scramble to reach the door of the room, Jess pushed past me, both of us gabbling and shrieking with fear, although we hadn't a clue what we'd do when we reached it. As we got near, the door slowly creaked open and, as it did so, the noise inside the room ceased abruptly.

What occurred next was beyond imagination.

A white, gnarled hand with prominent blue veins on the back came around the door and reached towards Jess's face, skinny fingers outstretched as if it wanted to stroke her cheek. It was the hand of an elderly person. Jess recoiled in shock, I dropped the poker and we both screamed and screamed, turning to race up the stairs to wake my husband. Jess and I had no desire to see what the hand was attached to, or what had been slamming around in the room.

We described what we'd seen and heard. Ted left us quivering in the bedroom and went down to investigate. He hadn't heard a thing until we'd started yelling.

Minutes later, he returned. 'I checked the room over and the doors and windows. All locked and nothing's been disturbed. The room is empty. I reckon a bird was stuck up the chimney.'

I snorted. 'More like an elephant, the row that was coming from that place.'

Jess and I sat in her room, talking over what we'd witnessed as we were too stirred up to sleep. Ted popped in. 'You know, I think it was your granma,' he said to me. 'She only died four months ago.'

'If Gran was going to come back, I doubt she'd have waited that long,' I told him. 'And why all the noise?

Jess spoke up. 'But Mum, remember what she used to do? She would often stroke my face affectionately.'

A chill went down my spine. 'And it was an elderly person's hand that we saw...' I said in wonder.

After that, Jess and I refused to leave the house for several days. The only doors to the outside led off the haunted room, and we had no intention of setting foot in there.

Eventually, the memory of the fear of that night faded and the family carried on as normal.

I'm determined to believe it was my gran in that room. Otherwise it's too horrible to contemplate what else it might have been...

Bertie continued to wander around the house, chucking the odd thing as usual.

We moved out a couple of years later – not due to the ghostly happenings, but because the kids had begun to leave home to start their own lives.

I don't know what went on in that property before we took possession, but I'm convinced that bricks and mortar retain memories of things that have occurred within the walls. Maybe Bertie had been happy there and simply didn't want to leave.

A few years back, a friend and I went on an organised ghost-hunt. The leaders had plenty of flashy equipment and gizmos, but nothing supernatural showed up. I have to say, I found it amusing. Because I know ghosts are real and that you don't need fancy gadgets to experience them.

Ten

All Keyed Up

We go on holiday for a little rest and relaxation – but Owen and his wife Meg got quite the opposite on their vacation...

I'VE HAD TWO EXPERIENCES I want to share – both, funnily enough, happened when my wife Meg and I were on holiday. Here's the first.

A few years back, we were visiting my cousin in Dover and chose to stay in an old, converted mill for one night. A self-contained apartment with a bedroom and en-suite bathroom, living room and small kitchen, it was charming inside, with exposed wooden beams in the ceiling and bare brick walls. Being February time, the weather was very cold.

Meg and I had dinner with my cousin, said our goodbyes and walked the few streets to our accommodation.

The bedroom was warm and welcoming and we climbed into the comfy, king-sized bed anticipating a great night's sleep.

I woke up in the middle of the night to go to the loo, Meg sleeping soundly beside me. The room was in total, coal-black darkness.

Knowing the ensuite doorway was on the other side of the bed over to the left, I got up carefully so as not to disturb Meg and made to walk towards the end of the bed. As I took a step, I felt someone push past me hard, like might happen if a person barged into you in the street. I felt the pressure of a body all down my right side and the push was so forceful it knocked my shoulder back.

I felt a rush of anger. 'What the heck!' I said to myself. 'There's someone in the room with us!' Groping at the wall behind me, I turned the lights on. I needed to find this person. My wife was asleep in bed, so obviously it wasn't her jostling me.

It doesn't take much to wake Meg anyway and the blaring overhead light along with me yanking open the wardrobe doors, peering under the bed and racing into the ensuite and out to the front door brought her round with a start.

'Owen, what is it?' she asked, blinking and shading her eyes with her hand.

I described the violent shove I'd experienced. 'But there's no one in the room who could have pushed by me,' I finished. 'The front door is still locked and bolted from the inside, so no one's been in or out since we came to bed.'

By now, I was starting to feel a little freaked out.

'Owen,' she said quietly, sitting up, 'something similar happened to me, about an hour after we'd gone to bed. I got up for the bathroom and although nothing touched me, I had a strong sense that there was someone in the room, someone brutal and unpleasant. I tried to wake you to tell you, but you were dead to the world as usual, so I gave up and managed to drop off.'

I blushed at this. When I fall asleep, it's like I go into a coma. Meg can shake me, yell, 'Owen!' in my ear and I won't wake up. I even slept through the hurricane that ravaged the United Kingdom in 1987, when I lived with my parents. Three trees hit the side of our house, the whole neighbourhood, if not the country, was awake and I didn't stir.

It's wonderful to be able to sleep that deeply – until someone I care about says, actually, I really could have done with your support that night.

We talked about the event some more then, being me, I went straight back to sleep. Frightened, poor Meg lay awake beside me for the rest of the night with the light on.

Looking back, I can see I'm quite chilled about the supernatural. I was far more worried about the possibility of there being a real person in the room, rather than some entity. That, to my mind, would have been far worse.

But I learnt my lesson about sharing possible paranormal experiences with Meg and wrecking her sleep.

The second alarming thing that happened was in Ireland the following year. Meg and I were over with her parents, Jeff and Annabel, for a family wedding, so decided to make a vacation of it and stay for a couple of extra days. We found a fabulous old double-fronted Georgian farmhouse with ivy tumbling all over the outside.

It was run by the farmer and his wife. We arrived late in the evening, and the farmer's wife asked the four of us what we wanted for breakfast next morning, running through a long list of the items that make up a full Irish breakfast. The four of us gave our orders: 'Yes, I'll have two eggs and sausages, but I won't have mushrooms, and I'd like orange juice not apple, etc' – all different combinations, very detailed.

I was fascinated because the lady didn't write any of this down and, as I used to work as a waiter, I knew how hard it can be to get complex orders right even when you do make careful notes. 'We'll see if we get everything we ordered,' I thought.

The four of us passed a peaceful night and in the morning, we went down for breakfast. It arrived, correct down to the last detail. 'That woman has an incredible memory,' I mused.

We went out for the day, came back late again, and told the farmer's wife we'd each have the same breakfast next morning. Then we all went up to bed at around 11.30pm.

There was a large landing upstairs. Meg and I had a room to the right, Jeff and Annabel were to the left and there were three other doors as well. Those other rooms were empty – we were the only guests. The farmer and his wife had quarters towards the back of the house, reached by a separate staircase from the hall downstairs.

At our room, I unlocked the door and Meg and I went in. She crossed the room to the sideboard by the bed and gasped. 'Owen, look at these,' she exclaimed, beckoning me over. There lay a huge bunch of keys, a ring with several large, long keys attached to it. 'They're like something out of an old movie.'

'They must belong to the farmer's wife,' I replied. 'But we've had a long day, we're tired and she's probably not going to need them this late at night. Let's hand them over in the morning.' So we ignored the keys and got into bed, leaving them on the side.

At around 1.30am, a noise woke me up which, as I've said, is almost unheard of. Cocking my head, I heard jangling outside the door, as though someone was rattling a big bunch of keys, along with other sounds. As I listened, the commotion began to make more sense and I realised I could also hear slow, regular footsteps. Someone was walking around on the landing clanging keys.

'What the hell's going on?' I thought and clambered out of bed. I wanted to tell whoever it was to go away and stop making that racket before it woke my wife. Unlocking the bedroom door, I went onto the landing. The minute I stepped out, the noise became fainter, as though it had quickly moved somewhere else in the house – downstairs, maybe. It was impossible to tell where it was coming from now.

Mystified, I looked around me, assuming the farmer or maybe someone else from his family was up and about. It was a working farm, after all. But obviously, farmers are normally in bed very early and up very early, and 1.30am was the wrong time to be up, even for a farmer. There was no one to be seen, but I could still hear the keys rattling. And then all of a sudden, a second door on the landing opened.

Out came Jeff in his pyjamas, eyebrows raised in alarm. 'What are you doing here?' he asked.

'I heard some keys rattling,' I replied. 'Really loudly.'

'Me too,' he said, grimacing.

I know Jeff well and he's a similar kind of person to me – reads a lot, is open to the possibility of strange things happening but isn't frightened by them. And is somewhat sceptical.

'Well, we're both up, so let's investigate,' he suggested.

Moonlight shone in through the window on the landing, giving us a tiny bit of illumination. Agreeing to leave the lights off so as not to disturb the women, the two of us started down the stairs into a well of darkness that was far from inviting.

Creeping around the house in the gloom, Jeff and I tried to locate the source of the sounds. We searched the living rooms, kitchen, utility rooms and pantry downstairs and up to the farmer's quarters. All the while, the noises carried on. They were everywhere, yet nowhere at the same time.

Jingle jangle. Clink clank. And those leisurely footsteps...

We found nothing.

'It sounds like it's in the walls – part of the fabric of the building,' I said, suppressing a shudder.

Jeff, sensible Jeff, was dimly visible in the shadows, the corners of his mouth turned down. 'Yet some, er, thing is walking around with those keys,' he said in a low voice.

Eventually, we agreed to return to bed, because we knew that if either of our wives woke up, particularly my wife's mother Annabel, and heard the noise, they'd panic and have us leave the place right then and there, in the middle of the night, which would mean sleeping in the car. Jeff and I were shaken but unharmed, so we figured the noise was probably the worst that was going to happen. We agreed not to tell Meg and Annabel until we were safely away from the place next day.

Back in my room, only then did I remember to check that bunch of keys. There they lay on the sideboard, innocent and undisturbed. Shrugging, I got back into bed and lay there in the dark. I could still hear that infernal jangling outside and waited to see if it came closer to the room again. It didn't, and eventually, sleep claimed me.

Next day, after the farmer's wife had brought our breakfast, perfect in every detail once again, I said to her, 'By the way, I've got a big bunch of your keys – you left them in our room yesterday.'

'Oh,' she said, 'I probably put them down when I was cleaning your room and forgot about them. I'm always forgetting things – my memory's terrible. I can never remember anything.'

'Hmm,' I thought. 'This from the woman who'd remembered our complicated breakfast order perfectly – twice.'

'The keys were locked in our room,' I persisted. The woman gazed at me with a faraway look in her eyes and murmured, 'Yeah...' Then she turned and went back to the kitchen.

After we'd eaten, we packed up, got in the car, and as I drove, Jeff and I confessed to Meg and Annabel about the relentless key jangling the previous night and our fruitless search for the source.

'How terrifying!' cried Annabel. 'I wouldn't have stayed another second if I'd known!'

'Oh my goodness!' exclaimed Meg, agitated. 'Why didn't you say anything last night?'

'Because we knew this would be your reaction and it wouldn't have helped!' I replied.

This event was very weird indeed. I'm open-minded enough to the point that I do believe people experience strange things. However, I try to find a rational explanation for them. But in both of the cases I've described, there wasn't one.

Our farmhouse stay is a mystery with a lot of unanswered questions. Given that our first night passed peacefully and there wasn't a problem until the second night, when the keys had been locked in our room, was there a link? Had the farmer's wife locked her house keys in with us, or were the keys to somewhere else? Being a farm, there were several outbuildings on the land and a couple of tiny, run-down cottages.

Had she locked them in with Meg and me on purpose?

And how come the two women, who were both incredibly light sleepers, hadn't been woken up by the din? Meanwhile I, who has the sensitivity of a log when I'm in the land of nod, had been disturbed by it, along with Jeff? Was it only audible to males, for some reason?

I had a feeling the farmer's wife knew we'd heard noises and was aware there was something in the building. Maybe she understands that's what happens in her house and she's kind of made peace with it.

I'm certainly not going back to ask, so we'll never know.

ELEVEN

CROWDED HOUSE

Lindsay contacted me to say she's 'lived in a house full of spooks all her life' and wanted to share her story...

MY MUM AND DAD bought this house in the 1960s. It was built in the 1800s and has that charming, olde-worlde air – honey-coloured stone and a bit crumbly-looking. I've lived here all my life with my parents.

It's a terraced house with very thick walls and three bedrooms. Being old, there have always been plenty of creaks and cold, shadowy areas.

I saw my first ghost here when I was about 11, in the 1990s.

I had a noticeboard on the wall in my room to the left of the foot of my bed, with my drawings and school photos pinned on. This particular night, I remember waking up at 3am and noticing the air was chillier than usual. In the dim early-morning light, I could see a slender female figure from the back who seemed to be stood examining my noticeboard.

At first, I thought it must be my mother. But this person was shorter and, as my eyes adjusted to what was in front of me, I realised it was a young girl. She had long ringlets down her back and a calf-length white, frilly dress.

My heart banging, I sat up in bed and cried out, 'Hey! Who are you?'

The girl turned and looked at me. She was about seven, with a sweet face, and reminded me of one of those classic porcelain Victorian dolls, with wide eyes and flushed cheeks. She wasn't scary. She gave me a wide smile, then – pop! – she simply vanished.

'OK, well that was weird,' I thought.

Although I knew I'd seen a girl, I couldn't quite believe it and wondered if maybe I'd been mistaken. It had to have been my mum, as the only other female in the house.

Next morning, while Mum and me were making my sandwiches for that day's school lunch, I said casually, 'Mum, did you come into my room in the middle of the night last night?'

Mum stopped slicing cheese to face me. 'No – I wouldn't do that. Why do you ask?'

I felt a bit silly and wondered whether I'd been half asleep – or going a teeny bit nutty. So I didn't mention the girl. 'Oh, no reason,' I replied. 'I thought I heard a noise.'

Nothing else happened in my room, so I put the incident to the back of my mind.

A few months later, my friend Susie was over and we were in my room sitting on the bed. To freak her out a little, as kids do, I said, 'Guess what? I've seen a ghost in this room.'

She was like, 'No you didn't – there's no such thing as ghosts.'

This was back in the days when TVs were big, heavy, angular boxes. I had one in my bedroom with framed photos and ornaments on the top.

'Really, I saw one,' I insisted. 'Last year, in the night.'

'You did not!' she laughed. We were giggling, then suddenly a china dog flew at us from the top of the telly, hitting me on the side of the head and landing on the bed.

We were rigid with shock for a moment.

I rubbed my temple where the dog had struck me, then picked it up and held it out. 'You can't have missed that,' I said. 'I told you we have ghosts!'

Susie found her voice and yelped. 'Yeah, I saw it!' she cried. Shaken, we hurtled out of the room and down the stairs. Mum had nipped to the shops and we were trembling, so we got a glass of orange each in the kitchen to steady our nerves.

'I think that ghost was angry,' I said, shrugging. 'But my

little girl ghost wasn't cross. Maybe this is someone else.'

'I don't care – I don't like this,' said Susie, frowning. Slamming her juice down on the table, she ran out of the front door and off home down the street. I said nothing to Mum and Susie didn't want to talk about it at school.

After that, I thought, 'Did I upset the ghosts by joking about them? I'll try being nice about them from now on.'

More recently, I was in bed early one morning. I was luxuriating in the warmth before getting up when someone yelled, 'Hello!' in my ear, really loudly. It was very clear. I jumped a mile, looking around the place. No one was there.

While there isn't a bad atmosphere in my room, there seems to be some paranormal link to it, although I never saw the girl in white again. But there's at least one more spook in this house – the main one, because he's often here. He 'lives' in the hall.

When you're in the kitchen, you can see through to the hall and front door. The position of the sink means that, if you're washing the dishes, you can catch movement in the hall out of the corner of your eye.

I first noticed the hall ghost a few years back.

I was alone in the house, washing up. I saw movement on my right down the hall and turned, thinking my dad had come in through the front door somehow without making any noise. 'Hi Dad,' I called. There was no answer, so I dried my hands and walked into the hall. It was empty. As I went back to the kitchen, I caught the shadow of a very tall man at the edge of my vision but, when I turned to look properly, there was no one there.

This has happened quite often when I'm in the kitchen and it still fools me. You think, 'Has someone just come in through the door?' but you look and no one's there. It's as though someone is loitering in our hallway. Someone who isn't real...

I thought it was just me who kept spotting this shadow. One day, I mentioned it to my mum, and she said, 'I've seen it a few times when I was in the kitchen. I thought I was losing my marbles!'

This part of England lost entire villages to the plague in the 1600s. I looked into the history of the area and, a century or two before this house was built, my road was shut off from the rest of the village in an effort to contain the plague and stop it spreading. The street is in the middle of a town now, but it was mainly countryside then. Apparently there's a mass grave nearby, full of the plague victims. Who knows what kinds of spirits haunt this place.

My mum has seen things, but not my dad. He's not a believer anyway.

I am. I think many of us are fascinated by the supernatural and the afterlife because nobody knows what happens at the end. And we want to know, to have that bit of reassurance.

My mum told me that the lady who lived here before us used to hold seances and was into the paranormal. Maybe that's why we have the spooks – because the seances dragged them back into being and they don't know why they're here.

There's one last thing. Long before I was born, on my mum and dad's first night here, they'd just gone to bed. Dad was asleep when Mum saw two people by the wardrobe, a woman and a man, leaning against the wall. The man was bald, with a thick moustache, while the woman wore her hair in two smooth rolls pinned back from her face. She said they looked confused, as though they didn't know what they were doing there.

Mum thought, 'Where did you come from and what are you doing in my room?' but she didn't speak to them. 'I tried to shrug it off,' she explained. 'You don't want that kind of thing in a house you've just moved into.'

Maybe I'm taking this too seriously, but I'm pleased I got to tell you about our hauntings. I'm sure the spooks will be thrilled to know they're being talked about in a positive way.

We don't think the ghosts mean any harm – they just share the house with us. Mum and I think they hang around the living room door, which is off the hall. It will creak loudly, then there's a bang, yet the door doesn't move. I always think it's the spooks trying to make their point.

I've decided it is what it is and, in a way, it's quite fun to live in a haunted house. And when the lounge door creaks while we're having a conversation inside, I think, 'OK, spooks, but your opinion is not needed...'

Twelve

Height Of Despair

*What had the hobby of two elderly ladies
left behind in Pammy's home...?*

I'd recently finished uni in Birmingham but, not
being able to find a job relevant to my subject, I was pleased
to get a temp position as a dinner lady in a local school.

A couple of the teachers rented a flat nearby in a
high-rise block on an estate and they offered me a room.
The paintwork in the flat was scuffed and the kitchen
hadn't been changed since the block was built in the 1970s,
but it was a short walk to work and the two lads I was living
with, Saul and Joey, were enjoyable to be around.

Being 22, I was out partying most nights, then up at
7am every weekday morning for work. Great fun, but I was
tired a lot of the time.

It was February and I'd been living in the flat six months.
One afternoon, I got in from school, switched on the
gas fire in the lounge and squatted down in front of it,

rubbing my frozen hands together. No one else was home. The warmth was making me feel drowsy – I'd been out, as usual, the previous night – so I grabbed a couple of cushions and a blanket from the sofa and lay down to rest by the fire.

The flat was still and quiet, and the gentle hissing of the gas flames was comforting. Letting my heavy lids close, I curled up and snuggled deeper into the fat cushions.

Then I heard a noise to the left of me, next to the fire. I couldn't identify it at first – a kind of swooshing. Opening my eyes, I saw what was making the sound. The door was opening slowly, as though forced by an unseen hand, the bottom scraping along the carpet as it went. It sped up and the was a bang as the protruding handle struck the wall – pushed by no one, with not a soul in sight. Frowning, I was wondering what to do when, moving swiftly, the door slammed shut, rasping hard on the carpet pile.

I lay there for a few minutes, puzzled. Had one of the boys come in without me hearing? Saul was a bit of a trickster. 'I bet it's him having a laugh with me,' I said to myself. Ha! Well, I wasn't scared. I'd show him.

Standing up, I threw off the rug, pulled the door open and looked in each of the rooms in turn – my bedroom, Saul's, Joey's, the kitchen and the bathroom. 'Saul? Joey?' I called.

Silence. I was definitely the only person here.

Half an hour later, the boys came in. I confronted them crossly.

'Have either of you been home in the past hour?' I asked.

'Nope,' replied Saul, walking through to the lounge with his rucksack.

'Double nope,' said Joey. 'We left together at 7.30am, had lunch in the dinner hall – served by you, if you remember – then took the afternoon's classes. And here we are. Why?'

'Because when I was having a nap in the lounge, someone opened the door slowly, then slammed it shut. Which is a mean trick to play on a girl on her own in a flat.'

Was Joey looking shifty? The odd expression I thought I'd seen on his face disappeared and he grinned at me. 'Neither of us would do that. We're the good guys. Me and Saul take care of the ladies, not freak them out. That wouldn't be good for our reputation now, would it?'

He turned to the kitchen on his left, opening a carrier bag. 'You were probably half asleep and dreamed it, Pammy. Anyway, I got us a chocolate cake. That'll take your mind off misbehaving doors. Come on, Saul – cake!'

I'd studied English at uni and wanted to write short stories for magazines. I'd bang them out and post them to editors but had yet to get one accepted. This being the early 1990s, I had a typewriter and it always had a piece of paper in it with my current effort.

I had the biggest bedroom in the flat, by the lounge, although I only had a single bed. My desk was over in the corner, to the left of the bed, and I hadn't been able to face my typewriter in weeks. Not since my last rejection slip, for a story I thought showed real promise, too! I'd probably been in the middle of writing something but, to be honest, I'd knocked out so many they were all blurring together.

One Thursday, I'd had the day off and, unusually, hadn't been out that evening, so I wasn't particularly tired when I went to bed. Leaving Saul and Joey watching TV, I settled down for the night, and, even so, fell asleep quickly.

Then I woke with a start, feeling disorientated, and at first, I couldn't work out where I was.

I seemed to be stretched out horizontally in the air, face down, my long nightie hanging down from my chest while my tummy and legs felt cold, so cold, exposed to the night air in the chilly room. My shoulder-length hair hung down either side of my cheeks and temples and my hands rested loosely by my thighs.

It took me a few seconds to realise that I was floating in a corner of my room, above my desk and the typewriter. Below me, the silver lever used to move the carriage to the right once you'd typed a row of words glinted in what little light there was in the room.

So this was an out-of-the-body thing. Weren't you supposed to feel calm, serene even, during these? I can tell you, I didn't. This was the worst event of my life so far. I felt terrified.

Could I move around? No – I could only hover where I'd woken up, near the window just below the ceiling. My fingers wiggled when I tried them but my arms and legs were pretty much immobile. I found I could move my neck a little.

And see the bed, to my right.

There was my head on the white pillow, face towards me, dark hair fanning out behind. Oh my goodness – was I dead? Was that what this was? So much for the worst event of my life. It seemed I had no more life left.

Tears bubbled up in my throat, but I couldn't cry – my eyes remained stubbornly dry. It was Mum's birthday in two weeks and me, Dad, and my brother and sister had a special meal planned to surprise her. Instead, the surprise would come sooner than that – that her beloved eldest daughter had died. The thought of the misery my death would cause my family was beyond agonising. And what about my own dreams? A partner, a home and my own family, kids piling into bed with me and my husband on a Sunday morning, like we used to do with Mum and Dad when we were little. All gone, with nothingness stretching ahead. Forever.

But if this was death, then what came next? And how could I find out? Confusion mixed with the shock, sadness and fear.

Then – oh, relief! I heard the body in the bed breathing. In, out. In, out. It was slow and regular, faint, but she was alive. Which meant I was.

My relief soon gave way to despair. How did I get back into my body? When I'd seen this kind of thing on TV, the person was having a near-death experience, like an operation that was going wrong, doctors panicking around them, or they were trapped in a mangled car in a ditch. They'd wake up to find medics trying to save them and zip back into their body.

But that *thing* on the bed – I couldn't believe it was me, because I was *here* – wasn't dying, as far as I could tell, and no one was trying to save her (my?) life. So what was I to do?

I was stumped. Panic rose in my chest. Can you have a panic attack while floating above your body? To distract myself, I looked down at the typewriter, squinting, trying to make out the words on the sheet lodged in it. I could just about see the top lines above the rubber roller: *The Dream Spinner.* (That was underlined – the title.) *She was the closest thing I had to a sister but we didn't get on that well...*

BRRRING!

My alarm clock went off, and suddenly there I was, in bed, my hand shooting out as it did every workday morning at 7am to silence the racket. I was back.

I lay in bed and pondered on what I had just experienced. Or dreamed? Whichever it was, I didn't want to go through it again. Ever.

Grabbing the heavy jumper I used as a nightgown off the chair, I slipped it over my head and fished my slippers out from under the bed, ready to hit the bathroom before the boys.

Wait.

I had to check something first.

The typewriter.

It took me several steps to reach the desk – I hadn't sat at it for at least two months. I released the mechanism that gripped the paper, pulled it loose and read out what was on it.

'The Dream Spinner. She was the closest thing I had to a sister but we didn't get on that well...'

I felt subdued that day at work, but dishing out food to the kids and a few giggles with my colleagues meant that, by the time I met my flatmates to walk home, I was feeling fine, although a little apprehensive about going to bed that night.

We lived on the third floor, and an elderly woman I'd spotted on our walkway a few times was knocking at our door as we approached. Thanks to her bold dress sense, you couldn't miss her. I admired the effort she put in and hoped I would be as brave as her in my old age.

With a shocking pink bob and thick green eyeshadow, today she sported a turquoise kaftan with tiny mirrors sewn all over. She smiled as we approached, the unnatural regularity and whiteness of her teeth betraying the fact they were dentures.

'Aggie sent me – she's the lady who owns your flat,' said the woman. 'She was my best friend for nearly 15 years, but she's in a home up the road now. Her son manages the rent for her.

'She wanted me to do something for her. She forgot to. Won't take a minute.'

Inside the flat, she headed straight to my room with us following.

With surprising ease considering she must be 75 at least, the woman knelt down in the corner on the same wall as my desk, pulled the edge of the carpet free and tucked a small rock into a space in the floorboards, murmuring to herself as she did so. Then she repositioned the carpet flap and got to her feet.

'All done!' she said, as if it was the most normal thing in the world, and started for the door.

'Hang on,' said Saul. 'What was that stone? What did you do?'

'Aggie and I used to hold seances here and also do astral projection,' she said brightly. 'We'd both lost our husbands and it was a comfort – we could call our husbands up or travel out of our bodies to the astral plane to meet with them. But not every spirit we came across was friendly, so Aggie wanted to add a charm to the room where we used to do it, to make it safe for the next occupants. So I put a black tourmaline crystal down for psychic protection and said a few words. That's all.'

To my surprise, Joey said, 'I knew about this. Aggie's son's a decent guy and he confessed that, asked if it might bother us to live here. I said no.'

'You could have told us!' exclaimed Saul and I in unison, exasperated.

I made Joey swap rooms with me, but the flat was peaceful from that day on – no bad dreams for any of us and the doors all behaved as doors should.

I loved being with the kids so much that I trained as an English teacher. I write the odd bit of journalism now, about education – I'm done with stories.

My experience with that last one I started kind of put me off them.

THIRTEEN
SCHOOL'S OUT

The whole village knew about the old school, but they didn't let Sylvia and Dan in on the secret until it was too late...

'COME ON, SYLVIA!' SAID my husband Dan impatiently. 'Let's hit the motorway now so we can avoid the rush hour traffic!' He started towards the car, waving his keys at me for emphasis, while I fussed over the details of where we'd be staying for the next weeks with our builder, Jack.

Dan and me both worked from home, him as a graphic designer and me as a business advisor. I had a complicated, long report to write and for both of us, the kitchen renovations – the completion of which, as is often the way, was extending further and further into the distance – were driving us demented. Bangs, crashes and wallops eight hours a day for the past three months – neither of us could focus on our work and we were starting to argue. Not like us at all.

Jack had insisted that this time, the work would really,

definitely, *positively* only take another six weeks. So we'd rented a place in a village an hour's drive away – detached, peaceful, silent. Dan had a big commission too and we were desperate for some tranquillity.

I'd let Dan find the place and only glanced at the photos he'd shoved under my nose on his iPad. 'Perfect!' I'd told him absently, my mind on higher things, such as the adjustments this particular company needed to make for Brexit.

In the car, Dan turned off the main road into a wide drive, tyres crunching on the gravel.

'Dan, this is huge!' I said, climbing out of the car while he followed me. The detached building had three tall, arched windows to the side and a huge one at the front, next to a door with two stained-glass panels. 'It reminds me of an old –'

'School?' said Dan, taking my hand and leading me to the front. 'That's exactly what it is – a converted school, built in 1880. See the foundation stone up there? Proof!'

And there it was, above the front arched window – a red stone engraved with the name of the school and the date.

'Well, at least the renovations have already been done and we don't have to deal with builders' racket,' I said, taking the offered key from him and unlocking the front door. Walking down the wide, tiled hallway, we came to a grand room that looked like a school assembly hall, complete with herringbone-pattern wooden floor. A couple of sofas and a coffee table looked lost in the centre. Above us, the ceiling was so high the owners had fitted a mezzanine floor to one side with a waist-height glass balcony, so anyone standing there could see down into what was now the lounge.

I turned to Dan, who was smirking beside me, arms folded. 'How many bedrooms does it have?' I asked. 'And, more to the point, how much are we paying for the privilege of renting somewhere with three times the number of rooms we actually need?'

'OK, yeah, six bedrooms and three bathrooms is a bit excessive, but honestly, I got it dead cheap. Same as we'd be paying for a two-bed near us.'

'I doubt that,' I muttered under my breath, but said no more. Dan was striding about the rooms like lord of the manor – or should that be master of the schoolroom – clearly chuffed with getting us what he considered a bargain. And it *was* stunning. We'd treat it as a little holiday, get back to being the cosy couple we used to be before the months of renovations had begun.

'There better not be any ghosts,' I said, following him into an enormous kitchen. 'If I hear children's voices singing *Ring A Ring O' Roses*, I'm out of here.'

'Isn't that supposed to be about the plague?' he replied, coming out and beckoning me to follow him up the surprisingly ordinary stairs. 'This was built by the Victorians, so we're quite safe.'

On the first floor, I chose a fair-sized bedroom but Dan, having poked his nose in all the others, said, 'We may as well take the biggest room as we're paying for it!'

The main bedroom overlooked the school entrance. It had an armchair opposite the bed and two windows to the left with a chest of drawers between them.

Dan brought our bags in from the car and we chatted as we put our things away. I was by the window when I heard the crunch of feet on gravel outside. 'Ooo, that will be the boy from the village with the shopping we ordered,' I said, pressing my nose against the glass to look. I could see the drive gates, but the last few feet leading to the front door were hidden by the entrance hall roof. No one was visible. 'I'll pop down to let him in,' I called to Dan, who was hanging up towels in the ensuite.

Expecting a knock any second, I ran down the stairs, grabbed my purse off a side table and pulled open the door.

No one was there – but then I felt something push by me, as though someone had come into the house. Instinctively, I turned and glanced down the hall. Nothing to be seen.

Dan appeared, rubbing his hands in mock excitement. 'Is the bread here? I'd kill for some toast.'

Before I could mention being brushed past, there was a rap on the open door and there stood a boy of about 12, puffing a little from a fast walk, carrying two bags of food.

Thanking him and taking the bags, as I was fishing in my purse for change for a tip, I saw he was trying to peer around me down the hall. 'Everything OK?' I asked, putting a coin in his palm.

'Yeah,' he said, shaking his black, curly fringe, 'it's just that I've never seen in here. It was shut for years and falling to bits before a rich guy bought it and did it up.'

'Don't tell me – it's the local haunted house,' I said, trying to sound jovial.

The boy looked startled. 'I didn't say that. I'm not allowed to...' his voice trailed off and he dropped his gaze to the floor as he began backing away.

'Not allowed to what?' said Dan, appearing over my shoulder. Spotting my husband, the lad jumped, his mouth falling open, then he was halfway down the drive to the gate. 'Thanks for the pound,' he called, scooting out onto the pavement.

In the kitchen as we made lunch, I related what had happened with the boy to Dan.

'Let's not get carried away,' he said, laying cutlery on

the large table. 'Yes, this is a historic building, but I'm sure the renovators will have chased away any spooks that might have been hanging about. So much of this place is brand-new and I don't believe the rubbish about bad memories becoming part of a building's fabric.'

'What?' I said, surprised. 'In all the 15 years I've known you, you've never expressed thoughts like that. Where's this come from?'

'Oh, I dunno – just popped into my head,' he said with a shrug. 'Let's eat our soup and bread, have a stroll around the village, then do a bit of work before the evening.'

But as we stepped onto the gravel and I closed the stout door behind us, I had the distinct feeling that I'd let something into the house that shouldn't be there. For reasons I couldn't quite fathom, I still hadn't told Dan about the – *what?* – that had shoved by me on the doorstep.

The November afternoon was crisp and wintry. With whitewashed houses and gently sloping cobbled streets, the village was small, with just enough shops and a couple of inviting-looking pubs. After our walk, we each settled on a room on the ground floor that would be our office for the next few weeks.

With all the tall windows, the house was flooded with light in the day. But as night fell, it was a different matter.

The high, high ceiling in the former assembly hall meant that even with the lamps that hung down blazing with light, there were shadowy areas beyond the mezzanine floor you couldn't see into from downstairs. And as I passed through the foyer on the way to the stairs, I sensed anger, malevolence, resentment hanging in the air. And yet how can a hallway transmit feelings to you?

That first night, I was woken by frantic movement by my side in the bed. Eyes firmly shut, Dan was thrashing about, arms flailing as though trying to beat something off. Then he began to shout.

'No! NO!' he yelled. 'It was for the best!'

In all our years together, he'd never spoken in his sleep or behaved like this. It was frightening to witness.

'Dan!' I yelled in his ear, pushing at his shoulder. 'Wake up!'

Wide-eyed and startled, he sat up and turned to me, putting a hand to his chest. 'Sylvia, I've never had such a dreadful, realistic dream. My heart is banging. Someone was hitting me, over and over, with a stick. I think they wanted to – to kill me,' he trailed off.

I murmured soothing words and held him close, but I was worried.

Next day, he brushed off my enquiries as to how he was feeling. 'Fine, great, never better,' he said, striding off to his work room and shutting the door.

But I knew my Dan. His brow had been creased by frowns at breakfast, and I saw him glance over his shoulder on a couple of occasions. He wasn't his usual happy-go-lucky self.

He was pretty much silent over dinner later and while we watched a bit of TV. I was almost afraid to go to bed after the previous night. I couldn't shake off the vision of seeing my husband so terrified – even if it was because of a dream. Seeing him that scared alarmed me.

In bed, we switched the light off and got into our favourite comforting spooning position. Once Dan had drifted off, I extricated myself and lay back to think over our brief time in the house.

I gazed around the room, which was almost totally black, the nearest streetlamp being some way from our bedroom windows. I could just make them out, two dormers with blinds that had been added to the sloping wall. This obviously used to be an attic room. The armchair squatted at the end of the bed and the darkness somehow seemed to be thickening in it as I watched. Like a child, I kept my eyes firmly shut and willed whatever might be happening to stop.

I must have fallen asleep after that. Then suddenly I was awake again.

There was a figure sitting in the chair, face towards me. Although the room was dark, I could see it plainly.

A young man, with prominent ears, a thin face and light hair parted on one side. He wore a stiff-collared white shirt with a slender black tie, the end of which was tucked into a waistcoat. A black lapelled jacket covered the waistcoat. His hands were clasped in his lap and he looked sad and weary, as though he was carrying a heavy emotional burden.

Terror rose in my throat and I screamed, reaching to Dan's side of the bed to shake him hard.

My fingers clawed in empty space.

Dan was gone, the duvet pulled aside, bottom sheet wrinkled as though he'd got out in a hurry.

I turned back to the figure and gasped, chills encircling my neck.

It was Dan in the chair now, gazing my way. He was in the navy pyjamas I'd bought him for Christmas. His eyes were wide open, but glassy. He couldn't see me. My husband had been sleepwalking.

Which he'd also never done before.

Dan was fair-haired, yes, but there was no way I could have mistaken my 43-year-old husband for the youth I'd just seen. Was I losing my mind? Was I asleep?

No.

I switched on the bedside lamp, got out of bed and bent over him. 'Hey,' I said gently, laying a hand on his arm.

Coming back to consciousness, he started back from me in the seat and screamed in my face.

'I'm sorry, stop, don't, *aargh*!' he yelled, covering his head with his arms as if to ward off blows.

'What on earth is it?' I asked, catching his hands in mine.

Panting and gasping, he threw my hands off and struggled to his feet. 'It was like my nightmare yesterday. A man was smashing at my head with a thick stick, shouting, "My boy obeys me, not you. I'll teach you to mind your own bloody business."

'Then the man sneered and said, "Sir."'

Dragging the duvet off the bed, he continued, 'I'm not sleeping in here. Let's go next door. Coming?'

We decamped to the adjacent room and I went down the stairs to fetch us both a glass of water. As I passed through the hall, there was a horrible smell that caused me to scowl. What was it?

It came to me in a flash.

Sweat. A man's strong sweat, as though someone hadn't washed for days. And there was another smell mixed in with it – alcohol, specifically stale beer. The odour was stomach-churning – and horrifying. Where was it coming from? It certainly wouldn't be emanating from a-shower-and-a-bath-a-day Dan.

Padding over the icy hall tiles in bare feet, I felt anger and rage in the air again as I walked to the kitchen. It was like a cloud all around me and I shivered with fear, as well as from the cold seeping into my freezing feet. Never mind the water. I had to get up to Dan and, hopefully, to safety.

I turned back to the stairs and, a second later, found myself being pressed against the wall next to them by an unseen presence. A man's body, strong and heavy against mine, stinking of beer and body odour, hands gripping my shoulders. Then I half-sensed, half-saw a face inches from mine, reddened and contorted with anger.

This wasn't the young man I'd spotted upstairs. Although it had been beyond dreadful to see him at the foot of my bed, he'd seemed a placid, benign creature.

This was someone else. Someone dangerous.

I must have let out a cry as Dan came galloping down the stairs seconds later. 'Sylvia, what's going on?' he bellowed, seeing me with my back against the wall, hands up in front of me as I tried to push the thing off.

As Dan grabbed my wrist, the pressure vanished along with the stench and I collapsed into my husband's arms like a puppet whose strings had been cut.

Sobbing, I explained what had happened. 'Jeez, what is with this house?' exclaimed Dan. 'Let's get the duvet, settle on the sofa with a brandy and sit there till morning with the lights on. We're leaving tomorrow. I can't take another day in this place.'

Having had no sleep, we were both exhausted by the time thin morning sun streamed through the windows. I texted a surprised Jack to say we'd be home by the time he arrived tomorrow.

Today was Sunday and, even though it was cold out, I left the front door ajar (in case we needed to make a run for it, if I'm honest) while I packed our kitchen things. Dan was busy packing up the studies.

I was putting pans in a cardboard box when a shadow fell across the kitchen doorway. Immediately, my heart began to thump. 'Not again,' I thought. 'Please, leave us alone! Let us go!'

The shadow withdrew.

Trembling, I went to the doorway. The boy from Friday stood in the hall, looking guilty.

'Sorry – I saw your door was open,' he said. 'You're leaving then. I thought you would.'

I walked towards him. 'Why are you here?' I asked. 'Is there something you want to tell us?'

'Yes,' he sighed. 'We all know the story of the school. In the village. My dad is mates with the bloke it belongs to and Dad told me not to say anything. Dad's a property developer.

'Most people are fine here anyway,' he went on, putting his hands in his tracksuit bottom pockets. 'But as soon as I saw your husband, I knew there'd be trouble.'

'You're not making sense,' I said as Dan, hearing voices, came over.

The boy nodded at Dan. 'You look just like him – I've seen a photo. That's the problem.'

Dan and I looked at each other, then back at the boy.

'In the olden days,' he began, 'poor kids were often kept off school as the family needed them to work. This one boy, Edward, was clever and the schoolmaster here tried to keep getting him to classes, so he could maybe go into a profession. But Edward had a horrible, violent stepdad, a farm labourer, who drank. The man kept threatening the schoolmaster to stop persuading Edward to run away from his farm work and come to school, saying he'd kill him if he didn't leave the boy alone.

'The schoolmaster ignored the threats and carried on encouraging Edward. Then one afternoon, dead drunk, Edward's stepdad carried through on his threat. He banged on this door' – the boy gestured towards the front door – 'and when a lady teacher opened it, he shoved her out of the way, stormed in and clubbed the master to death in the hall. He died about where we're standing.'

Grimacing, Dan and I both took a step back.

'From what I've heard, which isn't much, there used to be hauntings here years ago, but the only bad thing that's happened recently was when another couple rented it and the man was blond. Maybe two years back? He had really bad nightmares and stuff and there was a vile stink in the house, so they told the woman at the post office. They left after a few days.'

I was grateful to the lad for clearing the mystery up, but decided I wasn't about to tell him our business for the village to gossip about. Dan looked shaken.

The boy put his head on one side enquiringly. 'So what kicked off with you then? You both look knackered.'

Dan opened his mouth to speak but I cut in. 'Absolutely nothing,' I said with a smile that didn't make it to my eyes. 'There's a problem with our builders that's giving us sleepless nights and we have to get back. That's all.'

I went to the door and indicated to the boy that he should leave. I could see the disbelief on his face as I showed him out.

'Thanks for telling us the story of the school, anyway,' I said. 'What's your name? I'll tell the owner we met you and that you've been really helpful.'

'My name?' repeated the boy.

'It's Edward. Same as my great-great grandad.'

Fourteen

Up In Smoke

Given that Ryan's place of work used to be a funeral parlour, it's no surprise there was something strange afoot...

I'M NOT ONE FOR spooks and spectres. Even so, a couple of things have happened to me that I can't explain. I'll tell you about them. Then you can make up your own mind.

The first was quite a few years back, when I was 17.

After leaving school, my first job was helping the mechanics service and repair cars at a garage near my house in Blackpool.

This garage used to be a funeral director's premises. It was a big, detached house with two storeys that had been converted into offices and a wide staircase ran from the bottom of the building to the top floor rooms. The ground floor had a side door to the right that led to two large rooms side by side, which we used as our storeroom and workshop. We all knew that the storeroom was where the refrigerated mortuary had been, and where the mortician used to lay the bodies out to prepare them for family viewings and finally, the funeral. The viewings had taken place in a parlour on the ground floor of the house.

Out front to the side of the house, tall black wrought iron gates led into a huge yard that would fit at least four cars. This was where the funeral people would wash and buff the cars, ready to transport the dead to their final resting place. As you stood in the yard with your back to the gates, in front of you were two heavy wooden swing doors, like barn doors, that led to the workshop, where I spent most of my time. I guess the swing doors were to make it easy to push out a trolley containing the heavy coffin with its grisly contents. The storeroom was to the left of the workshop, through a door.

I worked here for six months altogether. Part of that was over summer, but those two side rooms were always bitingly cold, even on a hot day. The cadaver fridges had been gone some years by then.

The other mechanics used to talk about how, when they were doing paperwork in the offices at the top of the house, footsteps were often heard tramping up the stairs but when they went to look, no one was there. Several spoke of how they'd switch the lights off after work, leave the house and lock up, only to see the lights flash on again immediately.

I never experienced any of this and anyway, I didn't believe in ghosts. I enjoyed my job, so I ignored the tales and got on with whatever I was given to do.

One afternoon, I was on my own in the workshop, mending what was known as an invalid carriage, a motorised one-person three-wheeled car. On the wall at the rear was a large mirror that was 6ft high and 4ft wide. We would position our vehicles so we could see the back of them in the mirror. That way, you could be around the car front and put your foot on the brakes to test the brake lights, which would be reflected in the mirror if they came on.

I was a couple of strides away from the mirror, with the little car in between me and it and my back to the swing doors. They were so weighty that they would bang whenever anyone came in, which was annoying as it made you jump if you were concentrating on your work.

I was fiddling with the brake light mechanism when the doors banged behind me. I gave a start, raising my eyes to look in the mirror to see who'd come in, as I normally did.

There in the glass was the face of an elderly man in his seventies, white and wispy, like it was made of thick smoke. Just a face, hovering at what would be head height, with no body. I couldn't make out any other colours, but the face was mobile, the muscles working as though it were alive.

As I looked, the mouth broadened into a smile. The thing was grinning at me. This happened within a couple of seconds, and I whirled around quickly to see who was behind me, if someone had sneaked in silently through the doors to scare me, which was impossible anyway as they were so cumbersome.

I was alone. When I turned back, the face was gone.

What had I just seen? My heart began to thump wildly and my hands shook so much the tool I was holding slipped from my grasp to the floor. Badly frightened, I sprinted across the workshop, giving the mirror a wide berth, and into the house to our staff room.

Theo, one of the guys I didn't know very well, was there eating his sandwiches.

'Everything OK, Ryan?' he asked. 'You don't look so good.'

'No!' I stammered. 'I've just seen the face of an old bloke in the garage mirror, all misty. And now I'm too panicked to work.'

'Oh yeah,' he said casually. 'There's a ghost in that part of the building. A lot of people have seen that guy. Always in one of the mirrors. I haven't had the pleasure, though.'

I didn't see the face again, but I left after a few weeks. The episode was terrifying and I couldn't relax at work anymore. Talking to you, I can picture that face in the mirror, with its scraggy white hair and awful grin, as though it was yesterday. That was three decades ago and even after all these years when I think about it, it makes me go cold and shivery.

The strange thing is I'm not really a believer in the supernatural, even now, although I know what I saw. I'm not convinced that people come back from the dead.

Having said that, I did have another weird experience. This was 10 years ago. I was married by then, with a little girl, and me and my wife Jill were driving home from my parents' house with our daughter asleep in the back of the car.

It was about 7pm, in winter, and it was dark. We were motoring through a village down a road that had terraced houses on either side when we came to a long brick wall on our left, about 20ft high and a good 40ft long, the edge nearest to us sloping down to the ground.

A woman was positioned at the centre of the wall about 1ft away from it, staring at it and completely motionless. Her back was to the road and she was totally white from head to toe. White hair pulled back, white face in profile, white garments to just below knee length, white stockings, white shoes. The whiteness was very vivid – not misty, like the old guy in the mirror. This was a stark, new-paint white and I could see every detail clearly.

My knowledge of history isn't great, but from movies I've seen, I'd say her clothes put her as being from the 1800s. She was a very old lady. There wasn't a pavement where she was, just a narrow dirt track a few inches wide.

'Look at that woman, standing there,' I exclaimed to Jill as we approached her. 'What's she doing? That's a strange place to stop.'

'Did she cross the road in front of us to get there, without us noticing?' replied Jill, keeping her eyes on the woman. 'Oh. Where has she gone?'

We passed her – then she was nowhere to be seen.

Yet there wasn't anywhere for her to go, and there was no way she could have jumped the high wall or run the 20ft on either side to reach the houses.

'It looked like she'd walked across the road and simply stopped,' said Jill. 'Maybe there was something there in the past she could have walked through, before the wall was built.'

We carried on with our journey, chatting about what we'd seen. 'She hadn't had time to turn and run across the road,' I mused. 'It was literally seconds after we'd passed her and she'd vanished. No one could have moved that fast, especially an elderly woman.'

Jill and I weren't scared – it was just a case of: what was

that we spotted?

We drive down that road often and haven't seen the lady since – we always look out for her. I researched the area online and there have been a few ghost sightings reported – but none mention this snowy shade. It seems Jill and I were lucky to spot her.

Or unlucky, depending on your point of view.

FIFTEEN

A RATIONAL MAN

Having breakfast at a London café, I got chatting to the guy at the next table and mentioned that I wrote about people's experiences with the supernatural. 'Really? I have a story for you about my old house!' he exclaimed...

MY NAME IS MARK, I'm an accountant and I've lived in this area for a while. Eighteen years ago, my wife Shelley and I moved into a house not far from this café.

The house was built around a century ago, an Edwardian property with three bedrooms – two large rooms and a box room. There was always a strange feel about the house and it felt slightly creepy at night – a feeling I've not had in other houses. Our twin boys, Noah and Ollie, came along after two years and we lived there for six or seven years altogether.

One winter evening, it was maybe 9pm and dark outside. I happened to be at the bottom of the stairs as I was about to walk up to dig out some papers from the box room. The top of the stairs was in darkness, apart from the light coming from the downstairs hall where I was. Suddenly I saw a figure move across the landing towards our bedroom, then she was hidden by the wall. It was almost like a silhouette, a white negative, but I could see that it was a woman in a bonnet and floor-length cloak. There was movement in the cloak as she walked – it was swishing, although I couldn't hear anything.

The sighting was fleeting and quick and didn't feel threatening in any way. It wasn't like you see in horror movies, where people jump out of their skin – I felt quite calm.

But I thought, 'Did I really see that?' It was very strange. I didn't know what to make of it. Had I just made it up, I wondered?

A couple of months afterwards, I started thinking about this event, wondering if it had really happened, so I mentioned it to my wife.

'Shelley...' I began. 'This is going to sound peculiar, but a while back, I thought I saw someone in the house one night – at the top of the stairs.'

Her mouth fell open. 'Good grief,' she said. 'What exactly did you see?'

I described the woman.

'I saw that too – three weeks ago!' she exclaimed. 'I

actually felt pretty frightened, but I put it straight out of my mind as I was sure it wasn't real. But if you spotted it too – what does that mean? We both saw her on different occasions and obviously hadn't put the idea in each other's head as we hadn't talked about it.'

You ask me why I hadn't said anything to Shelley before? I was certain I'd imagined it, you know. Rational people don't see ghosts in bonnets on their landing! And perhaps it was also about not wanting to acknowledge something that's a bit scary that creeped me out late at night in my own home. And so, yes, we discussed it then. Why did we both see the ghost round about the same time of night? And just once each? We had no clue.

Noah and Ollie would have been three or four when we saw this apparition. Not surprisingly, my wife and I chose not to say anything to them.

A year or two on, we decided we needed more space and moved somewhere bigger. The ghost experience didn't influence us leaving the house one way or the other, although sometimes late at night, I'd feel there was somebody else there who shouldn't have been. It did always feel slightly eerie once darkness had fallen.

The twins are 16 now. We were chatting about the old house recently when Ollie piped up, 'Yeah, Dad, we never told you, but we used to see weird things in our bedroom at night – shadows of people and stuff.'

'We weren't scared – we just got used to it,' said Noah. 'Being little kids, we took it for granted that this was what went on in our room, and it was OK.'

Shelley and I told them what we'd witnessed and they weren't surprised, although they hadn't actually seen the same lady. We all agreed it had been a very odd house.

We've been in our current home, a few streets away from the old one, for about 11 years and I do find it interesting that the feeling there is totally different – I'm really aware of that. It's not creepy at all, at any time of the night or day, and neither me, my wife nor the boys have seen or felt anything spooky at all, thank goodness.

Newsletter & Free Exclusive Novella

One of the best things about being an author is building a relationship with my readers. Your support allows me to keep writing my books and I appreciate that. So do join my monthly newsletter and keep in touch. There'll be subscriber-only content, true hauntings and fascinating facts, plus you'll be the first to hear about my new books.

As a sign-up gift, you get the exclusive novella *How I Wonder What You Are: A Ghost Story*.

What lurks in the shadows at Lukas's family home and what does it want?

When Lukas, Nicola and their small daughter Emily move to a quiet street, the family's peace is threatened when Nicola acquires a car, which resurrects Lukas's memories of his mother's death in an accident. Then Emily discovers a mysterious music box in her room and events take a sinister turn. As past and present collide, Lukas's life begins to unravel in ways he could never have imagined...

Visit my website tinavantylerbooks.com to sign up and tell me where to send your novella. Bye for now!

To My Readers

I hope you enjoy this collection of spine-tinglers. If so, please consider leaving an honest review on Amazon to help fellow fear-fanciers who are considering buying this book. Thank you!

Real Ghost Stories: True Tales Of The Supernatural From The UK Volume Two is the second in a series of real ghost story collections. Follow me on my Facebook page @TinaVantylerBooks, my TikTok @SpookyTinaVT or my Instagram @tinavantylerauthor for news and information about my stories and upcoming releases.

Next in the series for you:

TRUE TALES OF THE SUPERNATURAL FROM THE UK & IRELAND VOLUME THREE

These 16 delightfully frightful, bone-chilling encounters with the undead will clasp you in a cold embrace and include: The mother so distraught she couldn't tell right from wrong in *Death Becomes Her;* the terror wreaked by a jilted lover in *Full Throttle;* the merchant incensed by changes to his home in *Shop Of Horrors;* the nauseating stench that accompanied a ghastly guest in *Bedfellows;* and the disembodied head in the hall in *Visitors.*

Available from Amazon

ALSO BY TINA VANTYLER

HAVE YOU READ THEM ALL?

*Four books in the Real Ghost Stories series,
available from Amazon:*

TRUE TALES OF THE SUPERNATURAL FROM THE UK

12 brand-new, modern accounts of real paranormal activity you won't find anywhere else, including: A stroll in the park that turned to terror in *On The One Hand;* an anniversary break that almost broke a husband and wife in *Floored;* a dream home that housed a fiend in *The Bad Man;* the horror that waited below in *Going Underground;* and a reminder to be careful what you wish for in *Not In My Back Yard.*

TRUE TALES OF THE SUPERNATURAL FROM THE UK VOLUME TWO

TRUE TALES OF THE SUPERNATURAL FROM THE UK & IRELAND VOLUME THREE

These 16 delightfully frightful, bone-chilling encounters with the undead will clasp you in a cold embrace and include: The mother so distraught she couldn't tell right from wrong in *Death Becomes Her;* the terror wreaked by a jilted lover in *Full Throttle;* the merchant incensed by changes to his home in *Shop Of Horrors;* the nauseating stench that accompanied a ghastly guest in *Bedfellows;* and the disembodied head in the hall in *Visitors.*

REAL GHOST STORIES: TRUE TALES OF HAUNTED TOYS VOLUME FOUR

15 original true tales of toys gone bad and innocence corrupted, such as: The ghastly gift from a damaged playmate in *The Doll;* the demonic fiend that pursued a

family in *Memento Mori;* the diabolical package from a dead mother in *Ol' Blue Eyes Is Back;* the small visitor from beyond the grave in *David;* and the sinister mystery man in the photo in *In Pieces.*

One collection of short ghost fiction:

THE DOCTOR AT CUTTING CORNER AND OTHER GHOST STORIES: SPINE-TINGLING TALES OF THE SUPERNATURAL

Six ghost horror stories to torture your mind with macabre images that will send icy shivers rippling down your spine, including: The surgeon with a bloody secret in *The Doctor At Cutting Corner;* the horror unleashed by accident in *Heads You Lose;* the vengeful fiend at a lonely train station on Christmas Eve in *Nipper;* and the gruesome act that lingered on in *The Ancestral Seat.*

ABOUT THE AUTHOR

The supernatural has fascinated journalist Tina Vantyler since she was a (weird!) child. The fact her mother kept her up late watching classic horror films and took Tina on outings to graveyards rather than playgrounds probably has something to do with her obsession. Several supernatural experiences of her own, along with the terrifying testimonies of people Tina has spoken to, have confirmed for her that, as Mr Shakespeare said, 'There are more things in heaven and earth... than are dreamt of in your philosophy.'

Tina writes fiction and non-fiction about the paranormal.

Acknowledgements

To everyone who so generously gave up their time to share their stories with me – I can't thank you enough. You know who you are even though I can't name you! Many thanks also to Lis and Oliver once again for casting their eye over the finished tales.

Printed in Great Britain
by Amazon